Barely Surviving

Christina Stuebs

ISBN 978-1-63784-681-0 (paperback)
ISBN 978-1-63784-682-7 (digital)

Copyright © 2024 by Christina Stuebs

All rights reserved. No part of this publication may be reproduced, distributed, or transmitted in any form or by any means, including photocopying, recording, or other electronic or mechanical methods without the prior written permission of the publisher. For permission requests, solicit the publisher via the address below.

Hawes & Jenkins Publishing
16427 N Scottsdale Road Suite 410
Scottsdale, AZ 85254
www.hawesjenkins.com

Printed in the United States of America

Introduction

I wasn't always scared of storms. There was a time when I was a normal person who chatted on the phone during storms, cleaned the house, watched movies, and did the basic things most people do. After the accident, my life changed. Jake and I changed. My world changed. It happened in the blink of an eye.

Everything was great. We were the ideal family. Jake and I had two fantastic kids. We loved going on camping trips, bike rides, playing family games, chasing, catching, and tickling the kids. The perfect life.

One dreary, wet day, everything changed. My life, the way I knew it, became shambles. Everything I had worked so hard for was gone. Jake became a shell of his former self, and me? God, I was a mess. Correction, I am 100 percent a complete mess. It's been six years since that terrible day, and still I am broken. My sweet, wonderful Jake, well, he died two years ago at his own hands, not being able to take the pain from that fateful day anymore. I am the only person left in this world who survived that day, if you call what I am, surviving anyway.

Chapter 1

Callie

"Breathe, Callie. It's just rain. Everything will be okay. Just breathe," I said to myself. *Boom! Crack!* "Ahh! Stop screaming, Callie. You're going to make people think there's something wrong. Why can't I just get over this fear of storms? One-one hundred, two-one hundred, three-one hundred—" *Boom!* "Ahh! God, they're getting closer together. Breathe, Callie, count. One-one hundred, two-one hundred—" *Boom!* Crying hysterically with tears running like a fountain, I made my way to my basement and into the bathtub to hide with my blanket, my pillow, and a small radio. This had become my new regime whenever it storms, even for a little bit of rain.

This is me, Callie Marie Palet. I am a coward who sleeps in her bathtub in the basement when it rains. I miss the days when I was carefree and could sleep in my bed every night with my husband and not resort to sleeping in my tub. I miss the old me, the one who was happy, had a ton of friends, who laughed and smiled, who felt she deserved to be loved. I miss that Callie the most. The Callie who believed she deserved happiness and love was the forgotten Callie; she doesn't exist anymore. That Callie was lost the second that storm hit six years ago. Then she lost anything she had left when Jake died. Jake took that woman to the grave with him. Everybody always says, "You can't keep yourself locked up. You have to socialize sometimes. It's not healthy to be alone." The best one is when they try to give me the tough love card: "It happened, Callie, and it sucks, but everything happens for a reason. Get up, get dressed, and get your ass cleaned up. You're going out whether you like it or not because I can't stand to see you like this one more second!"

That's the drawing point for me—always has been. I kick everyone out, ignore their phone calls, and go days without any human interaction, minus my social media account or TV.

Believe it or not, I have a job, a good job. Interior design. I've designed expensive households, even some famous people's. My name is out there, but how many times can you look at somebody to get pity looks? Or hear, "How are you holding up, dear? I'm so sorry about your loss, Callie. Please let us know how or if we can help."

It's always the same: I fake a smile, say thank you, get my job done, and get the hell out of there—back home, where it's just me. I have tried to go out and do things I really have. It just doesn't interest me. I can't get drunk because I become an emotional drunk, letting out feelings and emotions that I otherwise keep buried. It's not like they're going to be able to help me. Putting me in a psych unit, medicating me, and having me see a therapist did nothing. I tried for two years after the accident. I came to the realization that my trauma, or PTSD, needs to be worked out with me, myself, and I. Not anybody else, just myself. I write my feelings down in a notebook. If I dream, I write the dream down to try to make sense of it in the morning. If I have a panic attack, I use my anxiety medication. I am doing the best that I can. I am surviving the only way I know how to right now. I am surviving because it's what I deserve for living and my children dying. I deserve to be lonely; I deserve to be hated by everyone. It makes me so angry when people say it wasn't your fault, Callie. It was in God's hands. Nothing you could have done would have changed it.

I begged for a miracle. I prayed long and hard for days and days. I begged God not to take my babies, and he did. Since then, the person I have become has no relationship with God. I am angry, I'm bitter, I'm sad, I'm lonely and worst of all, I'm here. I won't take my life. I'm too chicken. I worry about how my death will affect other people and their lives. I know they love me, and that's what stops me, the love I have for them. I don't want anyone else to hurt because of me, so I wait until the day my fate is sealed and see where it is I end up. If only it was soon.

Chapter 2

"Mr. Owens, if I may, we've contacted a Mrs. Palet in reference to the new design for the office. She's very well-known and came highly recommended by many. She's due to come in for her initial look today at eleven if you're available. Gretchen, can you check my schedule?"

"Yes, sir, right away," said Gretchen.

"Now if everyone would excuse us, please."

Nate sat down behind his desk, loosened his tie, and stared at his best friend.

"Damn, Lincoln, it's going to be a long-ass day. What have we got on the new restaurant we just purchased? Any new input on how we should set it up or menu preferences?"

"Nope, nothing as of an hour ago," Lincoln replied, laughing. "What are your lunch plans today, Nate?"

"I don't have any yet. Why got something else you want to bombard me with today?" He laughed.

"Nope, just checking. I thought we could order in and go over the blueprints for the arcade. They broke ground yesterday, so we got to get those prints finalized and turned in soon."

"Yeah, I know. I cut the ribbon at the ceremony yesterday, Lincoln. You really do have a shit memory, you know that?" He laughed.

"Hey, don't hate now. I knew you were there. I was just reminding you of what needed to be completed."

"Yeah, you and twenty-five other people today."

Beep.

"Yes, Gretchen?"

"Sir, your schedule is clear at eleven if you want to join Mrs. Palet for her initial walk-through today."

"Okay, thank you, Gretchen. That'll be all."

Nate sighed while rubbing his temples.

"Lincoln, there never seems to be enough hours in the day for me."

Lincoln laughed while slapping Nate on the shoulder.

"Suck it up, buttercup. You wanted to be somebody, and you got your wish. The only one better than you now is me." He laughed while boxing in his face with his hands.

"What the hell am I paying you for? Get the hell out of here and do some work. I'll see you at one. Just ask Gretchen to call in whatever you want for lunch, order me whatever, and we'll work on the blueprints."

"All right, my dude. Catch ya later." Out the door he went.

I don't know how in the hell we even ended up best friends, but, man, am I thankful for Lincoln. Without him, I'd be drowning in overdue work and be in over my head, Nate thought.

Sitting down, he went through his emails, sorting them from highest priority to lowest, answering back who required it, and deleting the ones that didn't require my attention. He caught an email addressed to and responded back to from Callie Palet. Out of pure curiosity, he clicked the email quickly and skimmed the contents along with responses.

> Dear Mrs. Palet,
>
> Bustling Corp has decided to renovate a few areas in our company. We are requesting a bid if that is possible with such short notice. We understand if you are unable to do so, but we kindly ask that you return our email either way.
>
> Sincerely,
> Bustling Corp

Dear Bustling Corp,

I am available tomorrow at 11:00 a.m. if this works. Thank you so much for your inquiry about my services, and I look forward to working with you.

Sincerely,
Callie Palet

To Mrs. Palet,

Thank you so much for your time. Bustling Corp looks forward to working with you.

Blah, blah, blah! Okay, another stuck-up, snobby bitch, Nate thought as he exited out of the system. Stretching, Nate looked at the time and fixed his tie, putting on his suit jacket and the fake nice-to-meet-you smile he gave everyone. Heading out the door, he pushed too hard. He heard and felt a thud along with a grunt. *Damn it, now what?* he thought. Closing the door, he looked down and saw a beautiful woman rubbing her forehead with her hand sitting on the floor.

She had the most striking light brown, almost caramel-colored eyes, with a full head of curly brown hair with caramel-colored highlights that matched her eyes to a T.

Gods, her silky shirt showed just the right amount of cleavage, which made me want a better look at what was hidden behind that silky material. Black dress pants covered what looked to be legs that went on forever and red high heels that could make me relive my childish fantasies.

"Oh my gosh, I am so sorry—" Nate proceeded to say while the woman on the floor held her hand up, cutting him off mid-sentence.

"No apology necessary. It's just my luck." She laughed.

He held out his hand, offering to help her up. She grabbed on, and he helped her stand ever so gently, not knowing how hard of a hit she had taken because it sounded hard.

"Please, Miss err…umm?"

"Please call me Callie. My name's Callie Palet. I'm here to do a bid for some renovating the company is looking to do."

Okay, this is interesting, he thought. *She's beautiful, kind, and isn't threatening to sue yet*. Nate arched his brow and held out his hand again, allow me to introduce myself.

"I'm Nate Owens, president of Bustling Corp."

Callie took his hand.

"Nice to meet you, Mr. Owens."

"Nonsense, please call me Nate. Can I get you an ice pack, a doctor, ambulances?" He quirked.

"Oh gosh, no, I'm fine. I've had worse, trust me. Nothing coffee and a Tylenol won't fix later."

"Are you sure, Callie? It was totally my fault. I wasn't paying attention when I opened my office door. I was actually coming out to meet you and show you around when I so graciously knocked you down with my door."

She chuckled like it was no big deal, shrugged her shoulders, and asked to see the space they were revamping.

Chapter 3

Nate

"So as you can see, Mrs. Palet, it's quite a large space we are looking to renovate. What I need to know from you is how you need the space and the numbers you're thinking it'll cost to do this area."

"Please call me Callie. Do you have a vision of what you want the space to look like, Mr. Owens?"

"It's Nate, and no, we really don't have any expertise in this area. From what I understand, you come very highly recommended, so I'm hoping you'll have an idea of what will look good."

"Yes, Mr.—I mean Nate, I'm sure I can come up with something to look fantastic in this space. Honestly, it's beautiful. With all the windows, I have the perfect amount of light to work with. As I took in the space one more time just to envision potential designs, I was impressed. It was a really beautiful space. It had walls of windows on one side and an amazing view of the ocean in the distance. Another wall had some original light fixtures that I'd like to incorporate into the new design, at least a couple, and the chandelier, it was perfect for this room, but if they were redecorating to make it more modern, I could understand why it wouldn't really fit. I can have some ideas drawn up and sent over by next week. As far as payment goes, I can assure you that my price is worth it. It will be pricey, but you won't find anyone with my expertise and outlook on things. I am, quite honestly, one of the best in my field."

"You sound very sure of yourself," I said with a smirk on my face.

"Well, frankly, Nate, I know my worth when it comes to my profession, and let's be honest, I know what people say about me in reference to the services I offer and the work I perform. Now if you excuse me, I have other jobs to bid. I will send my bid over to your office as soon as I have it drawn up. It was a pleasure meeting you, Nate. I look forward to working with you on this renovation."

"The pleasure was all mine, Callie. Please give my best to the mister of the house."

"There is no mister, but thank you. I'll be in touch."

No mister but goes by Mrs., I thought. The first thing I noticed about Mrs. Callie Palet is she flashes fake smiles. There is definitely something else there, like she has a protective shield around her to keep others at bay. There seems to be a sadness, but she masks it so well. She'd look just like one would expect from a professional trying to get the job. A part of me was very, very interested in getting to know her. I've been so busy with work that it's been a long time since I've been with anyone or had a woman spark my interest. I'm just deprived. I laughed to myself. Or just maybe, I'm supposed to meet her at this time in my life. My mother would be so ecstatic to have me settle down and give her grandbabies. What the hell was that? I laughed out loud and shook my head. I've never fantasized about settling down and starting a family with anyone before. I seriously, obviously need to get laid. With that thought, I headed back to my office to finish a couple of things before Lincoln showed up.

*****

Gah! The nerve of that man, Callie thought! *How dare he accuse me of being conceited, as if I don't know my own reputation. I may be a complete mess, but I take my professional life very seriously and strive to make every single client I work with as satisfied as possible, even if that means redoing everything I have put together. Believe it or not, I have had to do that a time or two. Both times were for spoiled rich snobs trying to prove a point that they were better than me. But guess what? I completed the project to their liking, and they had no choice but to give me the credit I deserved for the job. I'll show him, I'll get this job, and I'll do it better than anyone in my field!*

Chapter 4

Callie

Lost in my own infuriating thoughts, I failed to see the revolving door with someone already occupying it and go to step in as they were stepping out. Of course, just freaking fabulous! There goes one of the last gifts Jake ever gave me. With tears in my eyes, I started blinking rapidly, trying to compose myself in front of this stranger that I had just completely almost knocked down. I stuttered a bit, trying to get my feelings in check while clearing my throat and trying again.

"I am so sorry. Please let me help you," I say while offering my hand.

"How about you watch where you're going, you imbecile."

"I'm very sorry. Please let me replace the drinks you were carrying."

"I don't need your money. You'll trip and make me spill them on me instead of you next. Good day, and I suggest you pay attention to your surroundings from now on."

"Again, ma'am, I am very sorry, and, of course, I'll watch where I'm going now. I apologize. Are you sure I can't reimburse you for the damaged beverages?"

"No, now if you'll excuse me, I'm already late."

God, twice in one day. I moaned while attempting to wring out my very wet and coffee-stained silk shirt. I walked out, my head held high, refusing to let anyone see how affected I was by the ruins of this shirt. *I'll break down when I get to my car*, I told myself. Sure enough, before I even got to my car, the tears were falling as the memory of

Jake giving me this shirt as a gift the day I graduated from college replayed in my mind. It's like a video on repeat that only I can see, and it's full of pain, anguish, sadness, and misery for what I lost, what I miss, and what I so desperately needed back. I'm so thankful this parking garage is underground and nobody is around. I hate when you cause a scene and kind people feel the need to try to console you. It's so embarrassing. I pulled open my driver's door and sat down, putting my head in my hands and letting out what seemed like a never-ending number of tears. Tears of sadness and anger that I ruined my shirt, and I let the infamous downright sexy Mr. Nate Owens under my skin.

As soon as I looked up from the floor, I was surprised my mouth didn't drop open. Nate was at least 6'2" with sandy blond hair that was perfect, not a single hair out of place, and hazel-green eyes that almost looked different colors if I moved my head in a different direction. His smile was so sexy, with a mouth full of perfectly straight white teeth, and god, even his nose was a perfect fit for his face. His body, I could tell even with the suit, was chiseled to muscular perfection. When our hands touched, gods, I swear I felt a zing of static like enough that I almost jerked my hand back. What bothers me the most is I'm actually attracted to him. Of course, I had no other bids today, but that pompous ass didn't need to know that. I haven't felt attracted to anyone since Jake, and that was fifteen years ago that we met and started our life together. I will be avoiding him at all costs while working on this job. I just have to keep my emotions in check while I'm doing this bid, especially since he was able to prick my skin, making me so angry. I could have used a few choice words with him.

Sighing, I took a breath, wiped my eyes, and pulled out into traffic to head back to my sanctuary. Walking in, I took a moment to just appreciate my home. It was nothing fantastic, of course, but it was my home. The walls were gray, and there was a beautiful picture window in the living room that drew in lots of light. I put my keys on the ring and made my way to my room and to the master bathroom. I started the bathwater in my tub. It was a deep soaking tub with bear claws for the legs and had added jets for a little extra relaxation.

BARELY SURVIVING

Some days, this tub did wonders for my exhausted body and mind. Undressing and grabbing my robe, I went to grab a glass of wine and some candles. "Ahh, just what the doctor ordered," I said to myself, and I dropped down in the water and just relaxed, going over my ideas for this renovation and how frustrating today had been.

Chapter 5

Callie

It'd been a long week between negotiating and compromising on both Bustling Corp and my side, and I was exhausted. Meeting with Nate again to just negotiate was really getting on my nerves. I'm not sure if it's because he smiles so perfectly and always has a counteroffer that I swear he's testing my temper for or if it's just purely the attraction I'm feeling toward him. We finally came up with a figure that satisfied them and me. I made it very clear I will not be accepting anything less than the last offer I sent of $31,500. When you calculate my expenses for materials and anything else I need, along with the time and effort I will be putting into this project, that number is totally fair.

What makes this week even more frustrating are the dreams I'm having of a certain Mr. Nate Owens. I may have a messy life, but I am human, and anyone with eyes can clearly see that the man is quite godly. It really should be illegal to have such beautiful features for a man. I have only ever once had feelings of sexual desire, and that was toward Jake, so if you could understand, it was confusing for me.

Last night, I woke up panting from a steamy dream involving a hot kiss from the delectable lips of Nate. I had so many feelings of want, need, desire, shame, and embarrassment. I just want to do this job and be done. If I thought for a second I could get out of this bid without a single repercussion, I would, but this is my livelihood. I may want to be alone and single for the rest of my time on earth, but I can't not work. I'm not dumb. I have bills to pay, and without a steady income, I would be living on the street. I deserve that, but I can't do it to myself. I just have to stay focused on this job and stay away from a certain someone while I'm at Bustling Corp. Although that may be harder than I thought, considering the email I just received from the exact man I'm trying to avoid.

> Dear Mrs. Callie Palet,
>
> You negotiate better than some on my team. I am looking forward to working with you personally on this project. We should have dinner to discuss the future plans of this renovation in detail. I have asked my personal secretary Gretchen to please clear my schedule indefinitely in the mornings for the near future until this project is complete. I hope that you will be understanding of my need to be involved with a project of this magnitude. My company has never paid anything near this price for renovating.
>
> I look forward to seeing your ideas and how this project will look completed. Please respond back with a day and time in the evening that dinner would work out for you. Again, I look forward to seeing and hearing the ideas you have for the Bustling Corp renovation.
>
> Sincerely,
> President of Bustling Corp
> Nate Owens

I swear this man will be the death of me! How can I have dinner with him and pretend that I'm not attracted to him or that I'm not having erotic dreams of him? I face-planted my head into my hands and groaned. Why me? I never have any good luck, I swear.

Dear Mr. Owens,

I'm not exactly sure we need dinner to discuss the ideas I have for the renovation of your company. I am very professional and will email any and all ideas I have regarding this matter. While I appreciate your enthusiasm, I believe I can complete this project without having someone watching over my shoulder. I will email you shortly with some ideas I thought would look fantastic in the space provided.

Sincerely,
Callie Palet

That should do it. *Good thinking, Callie*, I said to myself. As I started preparing the email pertaining to my ideas on the renovation that I have so far to send, my computer dinged, alerting me of an incoming email.

Mrs. Callie Palet,

Unfortunately, that was not an optional request. If you want the job at Bustling Corp, we will meet in person to discuss the proposition and task at hand for this project. I like to be completely involved in projects that cost my company this much money. I kindly thank you for your time and patience in this matter. If you could let me know a time we will meet. Thank you, and I look forward to seeing you in the near future.

Sincerely,
President of Bustling Corp
Nate Owens

Ugh! This asshole, the audacity he has to require me to have dinner with him! I swear I would love nothing more than to tell him off. No, what you'd love to do is put his body to other uses, I heard my inner self say. Oh, be quiet, you hussy! God, I do need to get out more. I'm obviously spending way too much time by myself since I'm now having conversations with just myself.

> Dear Mr. Owens,
>
> If that is the way you are going to play things, then fine. I can do dinner tomorrow evening at 7 p.m. If you can send me the location, I will meet you there.
>
> Sincerely,
> Callie Palet

Keeping my email open, fully knowing he'd email back soon, I twirled my hair around my finger, a nervous habit of mine. All while thinking about where we'd be going and what I should wear. It's not like I've never been to dinner with a potential client or anything, but what I haven't done is have dinner with a client that I have a crush on. Looking down, I saw he had responded back.

> Dear Callie Palet,
>
> I appreciate your understanding in this situation. No need to meet anywhere. I'll have my car swing by and pick you up on my way to the restaurant. I have made us reservations at Mila's. I hope you like seafood or steak, as this is one of my favorite places, and I can definitely vouch for anything on

the menu. I look forward to our dinner tomorrow evening. Have a great night!

Sincerely,
President of Bustling Corp
Nate Owens

Well, that sucks. I couldn't get out of this dinner if I wanted to. Why won't this infuriating man accept an email with this information? Now I have to find something to wear and make myself look presentable, not flirtatious, yet still professional. I guess I could always call Layla. She's been begging me to call for the last two weeks. I love her, but sometimes, I need to be left alone. I know I need to let her in more, considering she's the only one who still tries to talk to me. It's not like my other friends dipped out and never spoke to me again. They just got tired of trying and receiving no answer back from me. I don't blame them. I would have stopped talking to me too. What's done is done now. No time to dwell in the past today.

Chapter 6

Nate

I didn't actually need to be so involved in this project, nor did I necessarily have to have dinner to discuss this project. Could I have just looked over her ideas via email? Absolutely. But I can't seem to get Callie Palet out of my head. It's like she has consumed my every need and every desire, and I haven't even touched her besides helping her off the floor. I should send flowers as an apology for that. I'll send a quick note to Gretchen to call the floral shop and get a bouquet sent to her address on file. I can't even seem to help myself when it comes to her. She is like a drug to me.

I knew I pissed her off the day of the initial walk through by insinuating she might be conceited, but I couldn't help myself. I needed to gauge her reaction. She was so stiff and guarded. I wanted to see if she would give me another emotion besides professionalism and to the point, and, man, did she ever. That sassy mouth of hers put me right in my place, and my pants definitely got a bit tighter. I had to go adjust myself after she left just to be comfortable enough to sit down with Lincoln and finish those damn blueprints for the arcade. I won't lie when I say I may have relieved myself in the shower while thinking of those delectable lips licking and tasting mine, among other parts of my body being worshipped by her mouth. God, thinking about her gets me hard again. I told you, it's like she's my newly found drug.

Lincoln thinks I need to get laid, and he's right, but I can't seem to make myself go find someone. I feel like I need to extend a little to her and see where it leads. Hell, after this dinner, maybe I'll be satisfied enough to go back to the way it was before I crashed into her, literally. I laughed a little at the thought of her sitting on my floor outside my office rubbing her forehead or the cute dirty looks she was giving during negotiations. I just couldn't help myself but add another set of numbers to offer just to see the way she scrunched her nose and glared at me. Maybe to anyone else, they would have been offended, but me, I was antagonizing her on purpose. She's quite frankly one of the most beautiful women I've ever seen, with her long brown curly hair and beautiful big almond-shaped caramel eyes. She's got legs that looked like they went on forever and a perfect curvy body. I groaned. Looks like I'll be fisting it again tonight; it's unbearably painful now.

I put on some sweatpants and headed for my in-home gym, burning off some of the pent-up energy I seemed to have here lately. Working out in my home gym is sometimes helpful, but not today, I realize. I needed to get out and burn off some energy. I called up Lincoln to see if he was up for a run and then maybe head to the batting cages for a bit. Of course, he was game. I knew he would be. The only time Lincoln isn't game is if he's with a woman, for obvious reasons. We met at our local park, and as we were stretching, I couldn't help but hash out whatever this was between Callie and me. I told him all about pretty much, giving no option but to have dinner to "quote go over the renovation details and ideas," to which he laughed his ass off at me.

"If you think that's going to get you in her pants, man, you have another thing coming," he said as we jogged side by side.

"You don't think I know that, Lincoln? But I couldn't help myself. It's all I could come up with to get her to see me again. I don't know what it is about her that has me. Let's see what is the correct word I'm looking for. Entranced?" I said as a question, and again, Lincoln laughed.

"Bro, get your rocks off with someone who's interested. Why are you going above and beyond to see someone who's obviously not interested in the way you make it sound? You need to just find someone to take home, one and done it, and bam, no strings attached. If ya know what I mean, Nate. Wham bam, thank ya, ma'am," Lincoln said while thrusting his hips into his hands.

"Lincoln, you're such a player, and you're lucky there are no kids here, or someone might call the cops on your perverted ass." Of course, he laughed. "I don't know, Lincoln. Maybe I'm tired of the one-night stands. Maybe I'm ready for something new. I have no idea what I want from this woman right now."

Chapter 7

Callie

After sending an SOS text to Layla and getting a call not two seconds later, followed by a squeal of "God, Callie, I was so scared. I thought you were injured or something terrible happened with you sending an SOS text! Do not ever do that again!" she showed up with wine, an extra-large pepperoni pizza, and about fifty dresses since she's a fashion designer. She loves to dress people up. I won't say that I love all of them. Some are way too risky for me. First off, I'm not toothpick thin, and second, I haven't been all that kind with my body in the last six years. I don't go to the gym or run like I used to, nor do I eat anything like I should. After Jake died, I gave up on keeping my body image up. Technically, there wasn't anyone to look good for anymore.

I began regretting that choice as I looked at myself in the floor-to-ceiling mirror in my bedroom. The dress itself was stunning. It was long all the way to the floor, deep green with a low-cut front and an open back. Gorgeous dress for the right person. "But I feel like I have a pooch for a belly and not flat like it should be," I told Layla.

"Bologna Callie Marie! That dress looks fantastic on you. I wish you weren't so hard on yourself, girl. See what I see. You look hot! Add some red lipstick and green eyeshadow with a smoky eye, and you'll be the hottest girl in four city blocks."

I threw my head back and laughed. "God, Layla, only you could make me laugh in a situation like this one." Tired of trying on dresses, I settled for the dress and slid into some comfy jammies before slumping on the couch, wine in hand, and sighed.

"Layla, why can't anything just be easy for once in my life?"

Sitting down next to me, Layla put her wine on the table and grabbed my hand.

"Callie, everything that has happened to you in the last six years is awful and horrendous. I'm not sure anyone else would have survived what you have, but damn it, you have. You are here, and you are strong! You are stronger than anyone, and I mean anyone I have ever met. Most people in your situation wouldn't have survived the loss of their children and then their spouse four years later. I don't know how you did it, Callie. But what I can tell you is I am so, so thankful that you did. I'm thankful you are here and that you called me because I miss you. I miss seeing you and hearing your voice. I miss your friendship. I just miss you. I know it's hard for you to let others in, and I understand your need to be alone sometimes, but give me a little, okay? Let me in more often than once a month. I may not be able to give you adequate advice on what you should do in your situation, but I can hug you and tell you what I think you should do or guide you in finding the answers. Now can we please talk about this dinner date tomorrow evening because I am dying to hear everything about this pompous ass, as you so graciously put it, that is ordering you to have dinner and discuss a renovation for his company?"

After rehashing everything that had happened, from meeting Mr. Owens and him knocking me down with his door all the way to this evening's emails and my erotic dreams of him, I finally took a breath and sighed. "I feel so ashamed and angry at myself. How can I have the desire for another man after losing Jake? I swore when he died that I'd never let another man touch me or feel anything for anyone ever again, yet here I am, yearning for a man I don't even know to touch me intimately. Ugh!" I grabbed a pillow, put it over my face, and screamed in it.

Layla grabbed the pillow and slapped me right in the face with it.

"Hey! What the hell was that for?"

"Because you are being ridiculous right now! Do you seriously think that just because you promised Jake that you wouldn't ever look at another man that your brain or body would cooperate? I seriously don't understand your logic sometimes! Not that I want to bring up any sadness, but should I remind you of what Jake's letter said that was addressed to you? He wrote, and I do remember word for word, Callie."

To my sweet loving Callie Marie,

I am sorry I'm leaving you. I'm sorry I wasn't strong enough to fight for survival the way that you do. The last four years have been hell for you and me. I know we said we'd fight through it together, but I can't anymore. I feel like I'm drowning in my own grief. It has become so unbearable that I can't even cope anymore with the pain. It hurts to breathe. Every time my heart beats, it feels like shards of glass being pressed into my heart. Losing the kids was the hardest thing that's ever happened to us, and I just can't handle the pain anymore, Callie. Please forgive me. Please don't ever doubt my love for you, my sweet Callie, because you have been the most amazing gem I have ever received in my life besides the kids. I wish our love was enough for me to hold on, but my reality has come crashing down tonight, and it's just time I end my misery and save you the time of caring for a broken man. I love you, Callie Marie Palet, more than I could ever show you. Please find someone loving and willing to shower you with all the love and happiness. You deserve the world and more. Please forgive me for leaving you.

With all my love,
Jake

"God, I read that letter fifty times that night, Callie. I felt so helpless watching you crash and burn for a second time. As your best friend, it was heartbreaking watching you crawl back into yourself and cut everyone, and I do mean everyone, Callie, out of your life like nobody mattered but Jake. He left you, and you decided to leave everyone else. I won't lie and say it didn't hurt because it did, but let me tell you something. I understood that you were hurting and that you didn't mean all the hurtful words you were spewing to everyone around you, that you loved us but were afraid of losing anyone else close to you or hurting anyone close to you, so you pushed everyone away. That was fine, but guess what, Callie Marie, I'm not going anywhere. Do you hear me right now? I'm not leaving you ever. I don't care how many nasty things you say to me or how many times you tell me to leave you alone. I will always, always be right here or a phone call away, and do you know why, Callie? Because you are worth my friendship, and you are worth my love. I agree with one thing that Jake wrote in that letter. You deserve someone who will love you and bring you the happiness that you deserve. That was the only sentence that Jake wrote that I was thankful to him for. You didn't do anything wrong. Do you understand, Callie? I know you hate it when people tell you this, but it's the honest-to-God truth. You deserve to be here, but not to barely survive. To bring your light to other people's lives. You deserve to be loved, Callie, and to find love again. Hell, who's to say this Mr. Owens isn't going to be the one to give you the world, huh? Now let's wipe our faces from these tears and have a good ole sleepover clad in matching jammies, romance movies, and gossip. Now pick up that wine, Callie, and let's cheers, okay?"

"I love you, Layla," I said while giving her a hug. "I don't know what I did to deserve you, but thank you. I can't promise I won't push you away or take weeks to myself still, but I can promise I'll try to let you into my life more often than I have been. It's been a long time since we've had a sleepover, but I think we can pull it off. To having the best, most amazing best friend!"

Our glasses clinked together, and our evening started.

Chapter 8

Callie

Waking up in the morning was hell!

"Oh my god, Layla, why in the hell did you let me drink so much last night? My head hurts so bad."

"Well, I thought you needed a night to release everything you've been bottling up and recharge your brain. You do know this is what best friends are for, right? I'm here for you to talk to, you know. I will cry with you or yell at you. I may even tell you that you stink and need a shower." She laughed.

"God, shut up." I laughed. "And get out of here. I'm getting in the shower now."

"Good, shave everything and get clean while I go make a concoction to cure that hangover."

"Ewe, Layla, no, that green putrid shit is nasty!" I have no doubt I looked like a child having a temper tantrum, stomping my feet and whining.

"Oh, knock it off, Callie. It's not that bad! You can't deny it makes you feel better really quickly now, doesn't it? Now go and get cleaned up. We're running out of time to get you ready for this date tonight."

"It is not a date, Layla!"

"Okay, you keep telling yourself that, oh sweet innocent one."

"I am not that innocent. I'll have you know, I did plenty of stuff with Jake."

"Mmm-hmm, sure you did, and you have children to prove it now, don't you?"

"Wait, why did you say it like that, Layla?"

"I have no idea what you're talking about, Callie. Now shower and shave. I'll be waiting. We've got a lot to do to get you ready for tonight," she sang in a singsong voice.

Now I'm annoyed. She said that like I totally wish I weren't innocent, I thought as I turned on the shower to hot and hoped that it would cure this hangover, so I don't have to drink Layla's cure for hangovers. Getting out, I wrapped a towel around my body and one around my hair, wiped the mirror, and looked at myself. I've got terrible black rings, darker than usual, around my eyes from my usual lack of sleep and this hangover. I'm not sure what Layla brought with her, but she'll need a miracle to make me look presentable. I laughed to myself. I quickly threw on my favorite and most comfortable pair of sweats and one of Jake's T-shirts and headed out to the kitchen to drink this disgusting garbage.

Layla had her hand out with the drink. "Drink it all in one long pull. You know the drill." She picked up hers and saluted me while slamming it down in one go. "Bottoms up, Callie. We have no time to dwell on this," she said as she pushed the bottom of the glass to tip up the top toward my mouth.

"Oh god, I'm going to puke, Layla! What the hell is in this shit?"

"I'll never tell. It's a secret recipe passed down from my grandmother to my mother now to me. Now sit down and lean back. We are waxing these eyebrows you've let take over the majority of your forehead."

"Hey, my eyebrows aren't that bad."

"They won't be in a second. Now hold still, will ya? Or you'll have two lopsided eyebrows."

"You're such a bitch!" I laughed.

"What are friends for, my dear bestie? What are friends for?"

After what felt like years, dramatics intended, Layla finally let me up, but only to throw a cape over top of me. At the same time, I heard a knock at my door.

"Who the hell is here, Layla?"

"Don't get your knockers twisted, girl. It's just my hairdresser."

"Umm, I don't think I agreed to cutting off any of my hair besides the eyebrows, you know."

"Oh, girl, I am well aware, but it would be against best friend rules to let you out of this house in my dress and this unruly hair. Besides, she's not really cutting any length off. She's just going to tame those curls a little so that they cooperate this evening, okay?"

"You are the absolute worst, and I won't be calling you next time," I mumbled.

"What was that, Callie? I don't think I heard you correctly." She laughed with an evil smile on her face.

"I hate you sometimes. You can be so scary."

"Muaahhhhh! I was made to scare you and your little dog too."

"I don't even have a dog, you idiot!"

"I know. That's my favorite line from the Wizard of Oz." She laughed.

After two hours, her stylist finally finished and left, leaving Layla and myself to finish this look.

"I can't believe we've been at this for six hours, Layla. I don't know how you can do this all the time for these red-carpet events. It's one day for me, and I'm dying to get the hell out of here and relax. I feel like it's been a long-ass day, and I sat on my ass all day."

"Oh, girl, trust me, we went easy on you."

"Jeez, thanks, I guess."

"Now sit down and let me get your face on."

"My face, really, Layla? Now you're insulting my beauty."

"Girl, you know for a fact you are beautiful without makeup, but with the proper amount and highlights of certain areas, you will be perfect and absolutely gorgeous."

"Fine." I puffed out a breath of air, making my cheeks inflate, just to prove a point that I was annoyed and irritable.

"Okay. Callie, let's get into the gown. I'm so excited for you to see yourself," Layla squealed.

Layla helped me into the dress and got it settled perfectly.

"Wow, Callie! Just wow, girl, is all I have! You are absolutely stunning! If this guy isn't all over you tonight, then he is blind as a bat, Callie Marie."

"Don't say that, Layla! I don't want him all over me. I don't want anyone all over me. It's just a business dinner to discuss renovation plans," I said. "That's all."

"You keep saying that, but what about the dreams you keep having about him, hmm?"

"Those are exactly as you said, Layla, dreams, and dreams only. No actions will be taken toward those dreams."

"Whatever you say, girl. I'm just saying you look freaking hot, and I'd date you if girls were my thing," she said with a quick shoulder shrug.

I laughed and gave her a quick hug. "Thank you, Layla, for everything today. You really are a fantastic best friend, and I owe you big time."

"You definitely owe me, and trust me, Callie Marie, I will be cashing in on that very soon in the form of best friend time out and about on the town."

That's what I was afraid of, I thought, but I didn't dare say it out loud. I will do whatever she asks of me. I really did mean it. She's a fantastic friend to me, and I can't say I've been the same kind of friend to her. "I promise, Layla, I'm going to be a better friend for you. One that you deserve."

"Girl, you already are the best friend a girl could ever ask for. I love you always. Now I have to go, and I expect full details on tonight's date, I mean, business meeting, got it?"

Chapter 9

Callie

I wish Layla had stayed until after he got here. My anxiety over this dinner was skyrocketing out of control. I should message him and say I'm sick. Yeah, that's what I'll do. Surely, he can't fault someone if they're sick, right?

I got out my laptop and proceeded to open it up. Right as my email was opening, my bell rang, and I froze in place. Maybe if I just stay in one spot and don't make a sound, he'll go away. The doorbell rang again, and still I stayed in place. Again, the doorbell rang, and he knocked.

"I know you're in there, Callie. I can see the lights on."

Dammit, the lights gave me away. I hurried to the door, swung it open, and gave him my best glare. "How do you know a person who lives alone doesn't leave lights on so someone thinks there's somebody here at all times, huh?" I looked at him again and noticed that his mouth was agape, and he was staring at me like a fish out of water. "You might want to close your mouth, Mr. Owens, or the flies will get in. Now if you don't mind, I would prefer to get this dinner done and over with since I still have to finish a couple of things that also deserve my time. I was finishing a bid for another person when you wouldn't stop ringing my bell. I wasn't going to stand you up," I said while totally knowing that's exactly what I was intending to do the moment he showed up.

"Well, my oh my, Callie, you look, umm," he said while snapping his fingers, "there aren't even words for how beautiful you look. Green is your color, and it totally suits you. You are extremely gorgeous in that dress. I'm not exactly sure we'll get anything done with all eyes on you."

"Well, thank you very much for the compliment, Mr. Owens—"

"Nate, please," he said.

"Fine, Nate. However, can we keep it professional, please?"

"Absolutely, I thought I was being professional."

"Okay, shall we then?" I asked.

"I guess we shall, Mrs. Callie Palet."

"Stop calling me that. It's Callie. I'm professional, but not so much that you can't use my first name."

Nate

As we got to the car, my driver was ready, with the door open and waiting for us.

"Thank you, George," I said while offering my hand to assist Callie into the car. Closing the door, I looked to George, who let out a low whistle.

"Wow, sir, she's stunning."

"She is, isn't she? And completely off limits, understand?"

George put his hands up in surrender. "No competition from me, sir. I was just stating facts."

"No worries, George, just putting it out there."

"She yours, boss?"

"Not yet, but I'm working on that. We better get going. Seems Mrs. Palet has little patience for me using her time."

George opened the back driver's door, letting me climb in.

"Everybody fastened in and ready to go?" he asked while looking at us through the rearview mirror.

"Mmm-hhmm, ready as I'll ever be, George, is it?" Callie asked.

"Yes, ma'am, and it shouldn't take too long to get there with traffic being light."

"Please, call me Callie, and thank you for being the driver this evening."

I watched as she reached her hand up the middle of the seats and offered to shake his hand.

"Pleasure is all mine, ma'am," he said while shaking her hand.

"Thank you, George," she said before leaning back and looking out her window, pretending I was not there.

"So, Callie, I hope you've been able to draw up some plans for the renovation that we can go over," I suggested just to get her attention.

"Yes, Nate, I have several different options to offer you for your inspection and approval."

"Awesome. I really did mean it when I said I look forward to working with you and seeing your ideas."

"Yes, I understand, Nate, as I am very enthusiastic about this renovation. I think we can come up with something breathtaking given the views the space holds."

The last thing I want to do is talk about my company or this damn renovation, but it is the only thing I can use to get her attention. Pulling up to Mila's, George got out and opened my door so I could go get hers; however, when I got to that side of the car, she had her door open and was climbing out. How disappointing to know that she has no idea, professional or not, that a gentleman should always open a lady's door. I reached out and grabbed her hand, effectively helping her out of the car, and whispered close to her ear as she went to stand, "A man should always open the beautiful woman's door." I swear if looks could kill, I'd be twelve feet under.

"Well, Nate," she said with her teeth clamped down, "so if it were a date, but this is a business meeting, and that is it. As I understand it, I did not agree to a dinner date with anyone. Quite frankly, I was forced on this business dinner as I told you this wasn't necessary to go over some ideas and that I could have easily emailed you to have an idea or choice on what you wanted to be done to the space. If you by any means think this is a date, I think we should call this a night. I don't date. I don't have the time, nor do I have the desire to date anyone." I cringed internally as I said this, knowing that the words I was saying did not match the way my body was feeling toward this man.

"I apologize, Callie. I never intended to make you feel like this was a date. I was merely stating that a gentleman always opens the lady's door."

BARELY SURVIVING

"Now that we both understand that this is a business dinner, let's go discuss our business so I can get back home and finish up my other obligations, please, Nate."

Chapter 10

Nate

Dinner was going exceptionally well, considering the rocky start. She was fighting me with every twist and turn she could. I couldn't say or do anything right, and my god, it was such a turn-on. That sexy-ass dress and her sassy-ass mouth. I've never in my life been so attracted to someone or been able to get full-on hard just looking at someone until I met Callie Palet. When she opened her door, I was absolutely stunned. Never in a million years did I think she'd look so absolutely gorgeous. I wanted nothing more than to push her back inside and take her right there against the wall, but, of course, her sassy mouth brought me back down to the real world and out of my fantasies. When I whispered in her ear that I should open her door, I thought for sure lightning would strike me dead with the glare she was giving me. I'd never been looked at like that by a woman before.

    I knew I needed to take it down a notch when she told me she didn't desire dates or dating anyone in general. I took what she was willing to give me just to be close to her and breathe her in. Man, did she smell good. I'd never be able to stand another woman's smell again. I don't know what kind of perfume or lotion she was using, but I could smell it for the rest of my life if it meant it'd be on her.

    Snapping myself back to the conversation at hand, I saw her point to a certain picture of some fancy hanging chandelier, but what I was really focused on was the way her nose scrunched up ever so slightly while she tried to explain the vision she had for this particular chandelier and the blend of colors she wanted for the walls. She was the most beautiful woman I've ever seen.

All of a sudden, I heard thunder roll, and her body immediately tensed, and I noticed her start to shake slightly. She mumbled a couple of incoherent words before I actually heard something that made sense from her.

"Shit, not now," she said. "How did I not know it was going to rain? Please don't do this, not now."

All the while, I was watching her, gauging her reaction, trying to figure out what was happening with her and the small bit of thunder we just heard.

"I'm sorry, Nate, but I need a minute if you'll excuse me," she rambled and jumped up, nearly knocking our waiter down, stumbling down the hallway toward the bathroom, her whole body shaking.

Afraid of storms? I've never seen anyone react that way before. It wasn't even a very loud rumble, just a small boom. *I'll just wait for a few and see how she is when she comes back*, I thought. As the minutes passed by and she still hadn't come back out, I decided I should go check on her.

Knocking on the women's restroom door, I hollered, "Callie, are you in there?" No response, so I cracked the bathroom door and hollered again, to which I heard what sounded like sniffling and crying, but still nobody answered me, so I went in. I found Callie curled up in the corner and crouched down on her feet with her knees pulled up to her chest, face pressed into her legs, and her counting. After easing my way to her, I leaned down and gently called her name, and it was like I wasn't there, or she chose not to answer me. Hell, I don't know. She just didn't acknowledge me, so I tried again. This time, I gently rubbed my fingers across her cheek and softly called her name.

"Callie, are you okay, sweetheart? Are you hurt? Tell me what's wrong, please. You're too beautiful to look so sad."

She burst into tears, grabbed me, and pulled me tight.

"What's the matter, Callie? Please tell me so I can help you feel better, okay? I'm going to wrap my arms around you now, okay, Callie? I just want to comfort you. That's all."

Surprisingly, she didn't fight me. This was the closest she'd let me get. Selfish as it may sound, if she needed to be a bit scared for me to get to this place, I wasn't against it. However, I definitely wouldn't be the one to ever make her this afraid. After a while, I slid my hands under her knees and lifted her up. I'm not exactly sure she even knew what was happening around her or what I did, considering she didn't even react the slightest bit. I carried her out to my car and asked George to go take care of the bill.

"Callie, it's going to be okay, all right? I'm going to take you home now, okay? I've got you. You're fine. Can you tell me what's got you so upset? Please talk to me."

By this time, George was looking in the rearview mirror, trying to gauge what had happened, but hell, I had no idea myself, so I just shrugged my shoulders at him and kept trying to get her to say something, anything, at this point.

A few minutes into the drive, she started mumbling the names Savannah, Dustin, and Jake, asking Jake to please come back and why he left her. I was desperately trying to decipher the incoherent words, to figure out who the hell these people she was calling for were.

Then she started screaming.

"I can't breathe. I can't breathe. Jake, please, Jake, I need you!" and she passed out.

What the hell has her so scared? I knew she had a hell of a panic attack. My sister used to have them in college after she was almost raped, so I knew that much, and I could also tell her breathing stabilized, and her heart rate was going down since I was feeling it in her wrist. George cleared his throat in the middle of my thoughts, effectively bringing me back to the present.

"Uh, boss, what just happened?"

"Well, she just had a panic attack, George, but I'm not exactly sure why. I'm certain it has to do with this sudden storm, but I have no clue who she was mumbling about or why she suddenly got so scared, throwing her into a complete full-on panic attack." Pulling up to Callie's house, I searched her purse for her key. I watched her put in there and picked her up, bringing her inside. I laid her down on the couch and took off her heels and my suit jacket. I went into the kitchen to see if I could find a rag to wet for her forehead and to see if she had some tea I could start when she woke up. Her kitchen was extremely tidy and had a granite counter and stainless steel appliances. Her cabinets were painted a sea blue on top and a light gray on the bottom. I finally found the tea and started looking for something to brew it in, and once I found the teapot and got that started, I headed back into her living room, wet rag in hand, and laid it on her forehead. I looked around her living room and saw some pictures of a man and two kids. Both were brunette with brown eyes, cute as a button as most kids were. I decided to head back to the couch, which was one of the most comfortable things I've ever sat on. It had the puffiest pillows and soft gray material. I saw Callie start to move around a bit, and I rubbed my fingers on her cheek, softly calling her name as she came to.

Chapter 11

Callie

Waking up, I felt someone rubbing circles on my cheek, softly calling my name. I cracked one eye open to see Nate staring very intently at me. I raised my hand, realizing there was a damp cloth on my head, pulled it off, and sat up. I looked around, realizing I was at home, and my eyes got really big.

How the hell did we get in my house? And then it all came crashing back, which is what I could remember anyway. The thunder, me running to the bathroom, Nate coming in calling my name, oh my god, I threw myself at him, latching onto him like a crazy psycho person and sobbing into his fancy shirt. I have no doubt my eyes are the size of saucers right now.

"I am so, so sorry, Nate. I'm usually so professional. This has never happened on a job before." I felt his finger gently push on my lips, effectively shutting me up from rambling on.

"First off, you weren't at work. Second, I have no idea what the hell had you so scared, but I'd like to know so I can prepare myself in the off chance that it ever happens again. And third, you have my word. What happened tonight stays between the two of us."

"Thank you, Nate. I appreciate that. What do you want to know? I know you have questions. I haven't had a panic attack that bad in a really long time."

"All right, Callie, I definitely have questions. A lot of what you were saying was incoherent words, but some of it I was able to make out, three names you called out for specifically."

Wow, I really did it this time. He's going to fire me from the job now that he's seen how crazy I am. God, why did it choose to rain while we were at dinner, and why didn't I check the weather? It's so unlike me. I let myself get distracted by Layla and forgot why I hid from the world.

"Who did I call for?" I asked, already knowing the answer to this question but praying I didn't call out for the three missing people in my life I can't get back.

"Jake, Savannah, and a Dustin," Nate replied.

Crap! Crap! Crap! I don't want to explain this. Why did I offer to answer his questions? I should have just thanked him for getting me home and asked him to leave, telling him I was fine. How do I explain who they are without opening the door to a flood of questions?

"That's a loaded question, Nate, one that I'm not sure I want to answer and that I'm not sure you want the answer too."

"I'm sorry if I am overstepping, Callie. I am genuinely concerned for your health and safety. My sister used to have panic attacks similar to what just happened to you, fainting and all, so I know how much effort she put in to get better. Is there a way you could give me a rundown without the upsetting details that trigger your anxiety?"

"I'm sorry, Nate, but no. If you really want to know, I'll tell you out of appreciation for you getting me home safe when you could have just left me there to figure it out on my own."

"I'd like to know if you're willing to tell me, Callie. Maybe I can help."

"No, you can't, Nate, but I appreciate your concern. The reality is nobody can help me, and nobody can save me from my past. But I do believe it's for the best that I tell you the story since you witnessed an episode of mine. It's been a long time since anyone has been around me when it rains, let alone witnessed me having a breakdown. If it's all right with you though, first, I'd like to go clean up, take a shower, and put comfortable clothes on. Please make yourself at home, and I'll be out in about thirty minutes."

"That's fine, Callie. I've put some of your chamomile tea I found in your cabinet on the stove so it should be ready by then. How do you take your tea?"

"That's very thoughtful, Nate. A teaspoon of sugar and a drop of milk is all, please."

Shutting myself in my room, I threw my hand over my mouth and let out a sob. I raced to my cabinet and grabbed the Ativan, popping two of them since I had to tell this damn story of mine. If there were romantic feelings from Nate toward me, this would shut them down. Nobody wants a broken, sad woman. I turned on the shower superhot and just stared up into the shower head, letting it cascade down my face and body, hoping to wash away the feelings of guilt and shame I have for letting my kids die and not being able to save Jake from himself.

After a while, I finally decided to finish my shower since Nate was waiting out there. I'm sure he's not going to go anywhere. I've acted like a completely crazy lunatic, so I'm sure he wants to evaluate who he just hired to renovate his huge company.

Getting out, I wrapped a towel around my hair and body, went out to find my normal pajama wear, sweats, and a T-shirt of Jake's, went back in to brush my hair and my teeth, and made sure I looked at least somewhat put together. Before I went out, I took a breath and blew it out. I did it once more and walked out just to stand there mesmerized by the sexy god sitting on my couch, tie off, first couple buttons of his dress shirt undone, shirt untucked, and one leg crossed over the other with the ankle sitting on his knee.

If there ever was a god, I cursed him right now. I had to bear the worst part of me to a man who is unbelievably and undeniably one of the sexiest men alive. He should be in the magazines. Hell, he is in the magazines, Callie. He is one of the most eligible bachelors in the working industry, worth millions, no doubt.

Nate looked up, dropped his leg, and stood. It didn't take him but a few strides to get to me. He lifted his hand like he was going to touch my face but must have thought twice about it and quickly dropped it and placed it in his pocket.

"How are you, Callie? Feeling any better?"

"Yes, Nate, thank you for asking. Are you sure you're ready to hear my story?"

"I'm not sure I'm ready for anything, Callie, but seeing you so broken and distraught shredded my insides, so I need to know so I can try to help you."

"You're so kind, Nate. I've done nothing but push you away and be rude. I really am sorry if I caused you any embarrassment over this tonight."

"Callie, really, there was nothing to be embarrassed about. We are all human, and nobody is perfect. Obviously, something happened to you, causing you to have such extreme panic attacks, and I'd like to be the one to help if you'll let me."

Ha, I can't let anyone because if I do, I lose all I have left of my family. I'll forget the memories I've held onto. Hell, I've already forgotten what my children's voices sound like. I have to watch home videos just to remind myself of their sweet little voices, and that brings tears to my eyes. I felt a finger swipe under my eye and saw this man who barely knew me lean down so he's eye level, and he whispered, "Sweet Callie, one can only help if you let them in. Please let me in and let me help you. I have access to the best doctors and specialists there are. I'm offering you any of the help you want. All you have to do is take what's offered. No strings attached."

Does this man have screws loose or something? I wondered, looking into his eyes. I found myself leaning forward and almost brushed my lips on his before I caught myself and cleared my throat.

"Umm, well, you might change your mind after you hear what I have to say, so please sit and get ready for the sad details of my life. Just don't pity me or say you're sorry. You can't help me. Nobody can. Being sorry doesn't take it away."

Chapter 12

Callie

"Okay, Nate, this is hard for me to share, so if you could just sit quietly until I finish, I promise I'll answer any question you have when I'm done, okay?"

Nate shook his head, using his fingers to motion a zip it, lock it, and throw away the key motion, making me give him a small smile.

We woke that morning to rain and wind pushing our tent hard. Jake opened the tent and quickly realized we needed to get out of the tent and to a safer area. I was looking for my glasses. I couldn't see without them. Call it mother's intuition or whatever you want to, but I suddenly had this overwhelming feeling that a stick could hit Savannah in the head, so I turned around to grab Savannah's feet and pull her toward me, and that is when it happened.

When I woke, I could hear my husband screaming for help. I was dazed as I sat up. Something was holding the tent on me, and I couldn't get out. I reached to shake Dustin, hollering his name with no response. I moved his head to the right because he was face down. My hand was wet from what I thought was slobber. I reached behind me and tugged Savannah to me, put my hand on her chest, and gently shook her tiny body. She didn't move. I desperately screamed to Jake that the children weren't responsive.

I started biting the tent to make a hole big enough to get my fingers into it. I started ripping it so that the kids and I were exposed and someone could get to us. I hollered to Jake to call 911, that Savannah wasn't breathing, and handed her to him. I was trying to get to my son, to my sweet Dustin. I couldn't move him. I didn't know if he was breathing or if he was alive. I looked up and realized Jake was running around, trying to find help. I got up and took the baby from him and ran to the truck, where I laid her in the driver's seat, and attempted to give her CPR. It didn't sound right, sounded like there was something in her throat, so I opened her mouth and looked, but there was nothing. She was bleeding from her ears. I was screaming at this point, and I had no idea what to do for Savannah, for Dustin, for anyone. I grabbed Savannah, shut the door, and hollered to my husband that I was going to find help for the baby. I started running toward the main clubhouse they had for the campground. I remember my shorts being very wet and starting to fall off. I thought, just keep running. If they fall off, they fall off. I saw a truck, and I stopped running. I hollered help, and we both sat there staring at each other, I guess because a few seconds later, he just drove off. I started running screaming for help, heading up the hill toward the clubhouse, and heard someone holler, "What is wrong?" I didn't have my glasses, so I could barely see in front of me. I screamed, "Where are you? My baby isn't breathing!" At the same time, I heard sirens and darted up the hill, frantically screaming for help. They must have seen me because the next second someone, a man in a yellow raincoat, took her. He started breathing for her right away. Another person grabbed me and told me I had to take them to my campsite for my son so they could begin to help him as well. I took them to my campsite and hollered to my husband that I didn't know if the baby was alive or not. Jake told me to go find her and that he would take care of the rest. I started running up that hill again, this time looking for my sweet baby, my sweet baby girl Savannah Marie. I didn't know where they took her, and I was frantic, screaming, "Where did they take the baby!"

A lady screamed that they took her to the top of the clubhouse, so I darted up the steps and through the door. She was on the pool table. She had a breathing tube in her, and it was breathing for her. I was in a panic, screaming and crying at this point, desperate to know what was happening. A police officer came over and told me I needed to calm myself and tell him what had happened. At the time, I wanted to punch him in the face. Calm down? How the hell was I supposed to calm down? My nine-month-old daughter was on a pool table with breathing tubes. I had no idea what was happening. Nobody was telling me anything, and my son was at the campsite stuck. I had no idea if he was alive or what was happening. I was trying to pull together any strength I could find that could be left.

My life had been shattered in a matter of seconds, and I didn't even know what had happened.

My husband was driving the car behind the ambulance that was carrying our son. I rode in the ambulance with our daughter. When we got to the hospital, I just wanted to know where all my family was: my husband and my son. I was taken to my husband, and Jake started filling me in on what had happened.

A tree had fallen on our tent. I was in shock; a tree had pinned me and my two children in that tent. I had never felt so helpless as I did in that moment. It took the firefighters and emergency personnel thirty minutes to cut that tree off my son's abdomen. Jake said he was limp and unresponsive, that they picked him up and raced him to the ambulance.

I asked to see my precious Dustin. They led me to his room, and as I entered, I saw his Go, Diego, Go! underwear on the floor covered in blood. He was pale. I remember looking at his mouth to see if his teeth were intact. He looked perfect like he was sleeping, but so pale. His arm was hanging off the side of the bed. He was alive, and the machines were beeping and making all sorts of noises I had never heard before. There were doctors everywhere, nurses racing all around him, getting the doctors things they hollered for. As I was taken out of his room and escorted to my daughter Savannah's room, I spotted the man in the yellow rain jacket. I asked him if he was the one who took my daughter and initially began the CPR on her, and he shook his head yes. He didn't speak, just shook his head. I grabbed him and embraced him in a hug, sobbing yet thanking him for saving her and helping me.

I didn't realize it then, but he was obviously shaken and was crying himself. The nurse pulled me off him, and he walked away. I don't remember him saying anything at all. He was there and then was gone. They sat me in a chair outside Savannah's room, and it was then that I realized the tree had hit me in the hand, and it was bruised and sore.

I didn't care about me. I just wanted my kids, Jake, and my family to be okay.

A chaplain came and talked to Jake and me. He was asking us questions like was our son and daughter baptized and if we wanted to baptize them. He gave us updates that he could about the kids. I was panicked and in tears, hyperventilating. Jake said as he was coming out of the tent, the tree was coming down. That is when he started screaming frantically for help. He didn't know if we were alive, just that the tree was on top of us.

As I was trying to process all of this, I noticed the doctors had come out of Dustin's room and were whispering to the chaplain. I will never forget that chaplain's words to us. "I'm sorry to inform you that your son isn't doing very well. There's not much the doctors can do for him." As soon as those words came out of his mouth, the doctors all emerged from Dustin's room. I knew by the look on their faces that Dustin hadn't made it. That my sweet four-year-old son who loved being outside, riding bikes, watching his favorite cartoon was gone.

I couldn't breathe. My mind was racing. What had happened? Was I dreaming? I begged myself to wake up, for someone to please, please wake me up. My son couldn't be dead. He just couldn't.

I tried to stand but couldn't. I dropped my water and fell to the floor. I could hear my husband sobbing hysterically next to me, but I couldn't help him. I couldn't get up. I couldn't breathe. I didn't know what to do, how to get myself together, how to help him or myself pick up the pieces of our life. I didn't know how to comfort him. I just needed to wake up. I wanted to see my son. I needed to see him.

They took us to his room. Dustin looked perfectly fine, like he was sleeping peacefully. I started screaming, this was a dream. It wasn't real! I touched Dustin's face. I begged him to wake up all while my husband, my wonderful strong husband, grieved next to me, also stroking our son's face. I only wanted him to open his beautiful brown eyes, to hear him cry for me, for him to need me to make his little ouchies go away, but there was nothing but sadness, pain, and emptiness. I longed for my son to hug me. To crawl up next to me as he had a million times before that and tell me he loved me. I couldn't be in here anymore. I needed to escape, to wake up.

I was screaming and crying for my son. I left his room at that moment and have regretted it since. I left his small lifeless body and didn't go back in there again. I thought it was a dream, that I would wake up soon and everything would be normal. My kids are alive and not injured. My husband stayed in there for several hours. I couldn't function. I left my husband to grieve alone. I left my son in that room that day without telling him how much I loved him, how much I would have given to have him alive, what I would have given to bring him back, to go back in time to reverse the events of the day. I would have sold my soul to bring that boy back. I wanted to change places with him. I begged God for a miracle and didn't get it. I was so angry with myself for living, for not saving him, for not keeping him safe. I sat down with the medical examiner. She told me my son had died from hypovolemic shock. That his pelvis was shattered, his organs split, and that if he had lived, he would have never walked again. I was so broken, so devastated. Had God been punishing me for something? What had I done so bad that I deserved to lose something so precious, so pure, so loving?

I was so shattered inside. My entire body screamed with excruciating pain, raw emotion, from the loss, from the day's events. It was 7:30 a.m., and I was so exhausted. How could I be so tired? I had only been awake for an hour or so. I needed to put my focus on my daughter. I knew that I just couldn't get past my son had died. A tree had fallen on our tent and killed my sweet boy. I was sitting outside Savannah's room, just trying to process everything that had happened already, when a doctor came out and let me know they were going to be life-flighting her to a different hospital. I had just given permission when I heard Savannah's monitors go off. The doctor came back out and explained to me that she had taken a turn for the worse and wasn't doing well. I begged him to please go back in there and save her, to please do whatever he had to for her to live. I don't know how much time had lapsed between the monitors going off and the doctor coming out and going back in, but he came back and told me that her breathing tube had come loose and had moved around. That was what the problem was. They were able to get it back in place, and she was extremely critical but holding on.

Chapter 13

Callie

They decided that she was too critical to life-flight and had to take her by ambulance to the other hospital. I was told I could ride along, but if I couldn't keep myself together, they would be pulling over, and I would have to find a different way to get to the hospital because my daughter was so critical they couldn't focus on me and her. I had to keep myself together for her so I could be there. I needed to be there in case she needed me. I sat in the passenger seat of the ambulance with sirens blaring as we made our way to that hospital. I was so numb by the time we reached the next hospital that I couldn't stand up. I couldn't feel my legs. My body and soul were defeated. As they were wheeling me to a waiting room, I spotted my father and sisters. I had a second wind. I had support. It was at that moment I had reverted to a childlike state. I ran to my dad, sobbing uncontrollably again, and told him Dustin died. He sat there hugging me with my two younger sisters on the outside, hugging me and telling me he knew that he had heard and I was going to be okay.

As we sat down, my sisters began to ask questions. Everyone wanted to know what had happened. They had heard bits and pieces, but now they wanted to know. I looked around the room, realizing my brother-in-law, his wife, and his wife's parents were there as well. I was trying to communicate what had happened, but I was sobbing to the point of hyperventilating again. The other hospital had given me a mask in hopes that it would help.

As I was trying to slow my breathing with the mask, a nurse came to the door, clearly confused as to why I had a breathing mask with no oxygen. She let me know there was no oxygen going to that mask. I was finally able to get out why I had it and asked if she could get me an update on my daughter. My in-laws told me my husband was coming with his sister. Thankfully, my sister-in-law was able to go sit with my husband and make sure he had the support he needed because I was no help to anyone, not myself or my children.

When they first came to give an update on Savannah at this children's hospital, they told us she was a very sick baby and that she had numerous skull fractures causing fluid buildup on her brain along with bruised lungs. They couldn't tell us for sure if she would heal and be fine or if she would have permanent brain damage. There were too many what-ifs at this point in time.

I know there were a lot of people at the hospital trying to support us. I don't remember who or when they came. I do know that there was a room full that first week. I went outside with my aunt to take a break from everything when my body just started twitching. She took me to a doctor in the hospital, and they admitted me so they could give me something to calm me down. I made it clear that they were only keeping me long enough to give me IV fluid and the medicine to calm me down.

We didn't have any clean clothing, toothbrushes, deodorant, or anything at this point. My sister-in-law and brother-in-law went to the store and grabbed us some clothes and daily living supplies. My bra and shirt had Savannah's blood on them, so I threw them away as soon as I could. I realized the next day when I was showering that my head was extremely sore in one spot on the top. I had Jake take a look. He said there was a pretty good goose egg and that it had almost broken the skin. We had a CAT scan done to confirm that I was okay. For the first two days or so, we had a private room for our family and for us to sleep in, but as the days went, they needed that room for the next emergency, so we went into the main waiting room. We were shocked the first week at how wrong the news and media outlets were. They were reporting all sorts of stories about the accident that were off. One was that my kids were in a separate tent, which was so far from the truth. I was in the same tent with my kids and in the tent when the tree came down.

Neither Jake nor I could eat or sleep. We were living off adrenaline at that time. The doctors decided that Savannah needed a couple of shunts to try to drain some of the fluid to relieve some pressure off her brain. That night, the doctors had put two shunt drains in one on each side. Jake and I had taken the sleeping pills prescribed to us. I told her night nurse before I had lain down that if there was any change in the slightest bit, to please come wake me.

At 1:00 a.m., she woke me up. Savannah's pressure in her brain was building again. I tried to wake Jake, but he had a stronger dose of sleeping pills than I had, and I couldn't wake him. I went into Savannah's room and sat with her, talking to her about how much I loved her and needed her, and prayed to God to bring her back to me. The doctors came in and said they were going to see if they could detect any brain activity. After they hooked her up to the machine, they said they didn't see any brain activity at all but that it was early, and they would check again another day.

Her little body was so swollen, her skin so tight from all the fluids. She looked like a balloon, ready to pop. We had her baptized and prayed at her bedside constantly with priests, friends, family, and anybody really who was willing to pray for us and with us. Day six at the hospital, July 26, 2008, the doctors tested her brain activity, and again, there was nothing. They had decided that they needed to go in and remove a part of her skull to relieve some of the pressure on her brain. After Jake and I had discussed it, we decided to allow them to follow the procedure.

They moved us to a different waiting room. It was so cold in that waiting room. They had reclining chairs in there, so we curled up with blankets to start waiting for the doctors to come to update us on Savannah and how the surgery was going. It wasn't very long before one came to get us. He pulled us into a room and asked us to sit down. He began telling us that it was worse than they had expected, that there was so much dead brain she couldn't and would never wake up. That we needed to start thinking about removing life support.

I couldn't believe what I was hearing. I thought she was going to pull through. I wasn't expecting this. It was as if someone had socked me so hard in the stomach that I needed to puke. I hated God, I hated myself, I hated everything. I wanted a miracle. I prayed so hard for a miracle. I knew they had happened. You read about them every day. Why couldn't I have just one miracle, one damn break? I needed her to get better! I didn't want to decide to remove life support. I wanted to hold her, tell her it would be okay, that mommy was there. I would protect her from any more pain. Jake and I cried a long time together before we decided that it wasn't fair to keep her alive if she was going to be in a vegetative state for the rest of her life.

We made the most difficult decision in our lives. We decided to remove Savannah's life support. I didn't know how I was going to do this, how I was going to go on without Dustin and Savannah.

On July 27, 2008, my daughter Savannah Marie Palet was placed in my arms and her life support removed. I rocked my sweet girl and cried and sobbed and kissed her sweet face over and over for hours I did this. I asked for a bulb syringe and cleaned the fluid spilling from her nose as she was gasping for air. The nurses had soft, calming music. I handed her to my husband, went to update everyone, came back, and began rocking her and loving her for as long as I could. After four hours, I told her it was okay to go, that I loved her, and that I would be okay. To hug her brother and look after us here.

She finally took her last breath, and then I begged her to come back to breathe again. I wasn't ready. I couldn't do it without her here. I was such a broken person.

As the family started to come in, I realized my family, everyone had left, leaving only my father's sister and her husband. My husband's family, all of his siblings, and their spouses were all there. I watched them surround Jake and embrace him with support, comfort, and love. I had never been so jealous of something in my entire life. I had never asked my family for anything, nothing, and the one time I needed them, they left me. What had I done to deserve to lose my children and to have no support?

Don't get me wrong, I was grateful for my aunt and her husband, but I was so sad and disappointed. I was at my lowest point, and all my family had chosen to leave when I needed them the most. I had never been so angry, so filled with hate and rage.

I wanted to die. I wanted to suffer as my children had. Why had God left me here but taken them? I was in the same tent hit by the same tree, yet I was here, and they weren't.

I had no family, lost both my children, and had no idea what I was going to do or how I was going to survive. That drive back to our *hometown was long. I had taken so much anxiety medication prescribed to me that I fell asleep. I was exhausted. My entire life had fallen apart and crashed down around me. In seven days, we had gone from a family of four to a family of two, just Jake and I again. I had to plan a funeral. There were so many things running through my head. Where were the services going to be? How was I going to bury my two beautiful children? There were so many things details to figure out before anything could happen. The morning after Savannah's death, I woke up early, my heart racing, my mind replaying the events of the week. I couldn't stop the tears that started pouring down the sides of my face. Jake was asleep next to me.*

I was afraid I would wake him, so I decided to get up. Realizing my sister-in-law had an alarm, I went down the hall to ask if her alarm was set. I could barely speak, my body so shaken by fear, the reality of what had happened, the grief so overwhelming it just overtook my entire body. I was shaking uncontrollably. I wanted what I couldn't have. I wanted Dustin and Savannah back. I knew God had made a mistake. They were just babies.

The next week was a blur. I either had an alcoholic beverage in my hand or anxiety pills I was swallowing down like candy. I was fighting to survive the grief, to live, to get away from the pain I was feeling constantly. Picking the church for their services was where we had to start. When we went to the funeral parlor to pick out caskets, I couldn't believe how many there were to choose from. I didn't want to be there, so we quickly made our choices and left. I had to go fill out the paperwork for the headstone. My hands were shaking so badly I could barely write his name: Dustin Matthew Palet, born April 7, 2004, died July 21, 2008, and Savannah Marie Palet, born October 22, 2007, died July 27, 2008. I had a three-wheeled bike etched on Dustin's side of the tombstone and a baby doll etched on Savannah's side. I couldn't believe I was putting death dates for two of the purest, most loving souls I had known. My beautiful babies went before me.

I was brought a memory box for Savannah from that hospital. It had a ceramic creation of her tiny little hand, two certificates with her prints, her earrings in a small bag, the locks of her hair that had been shaved and cut before her surgeries, and books on grieving. We decided to play "Jesus loves me" at the funeral. I wanted to help Jake grieve to take away his pain, and I couldn't. I didn't know how to make this right or how to make it better. They needed me, Jake needed me, and I couldn't be there for any of them. I only knew I hurt and had lost myself. I wasn't their mother or Jake's wife. I was crippled by grief, lost in my own sorrows, unable to decide whether I wanted to live or fall into the black hole that had emerged. I knew one thing: I needed to get myself through the funeral.

I vaguely remember bits and pieces of the funeral. It was August 1, 2008. We had put Dustin in a suit with his favorite blanket in his casket with him and Savannah's blanket with the little doll she loved so much. I couldn't get over how normal my boy looked, no marks, no bruises. How could he have so much internal damage but look fine? Savannah didn't look at all herself. We got her a little dress with a bonnet to cover the incisions from all the surgeries she had. Her body was so swollen and unproportioned that it wasn't my baby, my sweet girl. I sat in the front pew with my husband, sobbing, trying to console my husband the best I could. I needed this day to be over. I couldn't take much more, and I was falling apart. I have no idea who drove me to the cemetery or how I got home.

Chapter 14

Callie

Everyone said my Jake and I would never stay together and that it's hard on a marriage after you lose a child. I had to do what was necessary to keep my husband, to keep my family, and to keep what was left of it together. We had decided that we couldn't stay in the home we had shared with the kids as a family and that there were too many memories we shared with them there. We stayed with my sister-in-law until October, until we found a house. I was so lost, so broken, and unaware of my surroundings. I didn't know what I wanted: to live, to die, to merely survive. I drank a lot those days. I went into survival mode. I drank alcohol almost every night until I was wasted and could no longer feel anything. If I were sober, I hurt. I could feel the grief I was forced to deal with the pain of losing the kids. I didn't want to feel anything. I wanted my life back, my kids back, to feel normal again.

That first year, I cried all the time. I'm sure people thought I was crazy. I could be cooking dinner or talking to someone, and my emotions overwhelm me all of a sudden, and I would be sobbing for no reason besides missing or wanting my kids. One day, I decided I needed to stop drinking, so I did. I wondered what I had been doing, what I was thinking, and why I had left Jake so long by himself with me being so irresponsible.

What had I been thinking? I hadn't been getting better. The pain was still there, the grief still so overwhelming it took my breath away. I started taking it day by day, minute by minute. If I couldn't stand because of the grief that overtook me, then so be it. I was not picking up another drink. I hoped my Jake could forgive me for leaving him without a wife that year, a wife who was present yet not. I wanted him to know I loved him and that he mattered too.

Trying to balance my grief and my life, my husband, and my job was so difficult. There were days I couldn't stand to look at myself in the mirror, let alone get out of bed or feed myself. I was trying so hard to take the days by minutes and seconds to survive until the next day.

Jake was my priority. I knew he was losing himself. I loved him so much more than I did myself. He deserved so much more than I was able to give him. I was a terrible mother, I knew, and they had to have known it. I so often felt as though my all just wasn't enough, not even close. I was severely depressed all the time. I was fixated on getting what I couldn't have back, all the while trying to make my husband happy. Making myself seem normal and okay to the outside world while my insides screamed what the hell are you doing? You don't deserve this life, your husband. Jake deserved someone who was whole and perfect, not broken and disguised as someone who was happy and whole. I knew I wasn't fixed or healed from the loss of the kids.

I was making sure everyone around me thought I was okay, that everything was fine, and that I was doing the normal grieving thing that I thought everyone was supposed to do after losing someone so important and special to them. I didn't know how to grieve, how long it would go on for. I was giving as much of myself to my Jake as I could, but I was still lost.

It had already been a year and a half, and I still couldn't pull myself above the black hole. I even fantasized about what it would be like for my family if I just let myself fall in. If I had let myself die, maybe, just maybe, they would be okay and could move on.

I imagined myself dying many different ways, never in my home where my husband would find me, but outside. A car accident maybe, so they wouldn't have to think I had killed myself and left them with permanent scars. Several times, I thought, just drive off the bridge into the river, you will drown, but it'll be over, or drive into the telephone pole head-on, and maybe you'll die quickly.

I never went through with it because of Jake. I didn't want him to be in pain, mourning the loss of his wife. I obviously always envisioned him crying, needing me, and me not being there. I did what I could to distract myself from the loss and the grieving I felt constantly. I wanted to be a great mother again. I wanted to love myself the way my kids and husband loved me, but I couldn't.

The survivor's guilt was so strong it overtook any thought I had that made me feel like I was a good person. I didn't want people to like me, to want to be my friend or love me. I wanted to be alone and suffer. As much as I loved my husband at that time in my life, I wished he didn't want me. He made it too hard for me to want to live when I wanted to die.

I blamed myself for Dustin's and Savannah's deaths. I should have gotten right out of the tent, but instead, I was looking for my glasses. Why were my glasses so important to me? Why had I not just gotten up and grabbed them and made a mad dash for the truck to get them to safety? Instead, I stayed and looked for those glasses that made it out of that tent that day and were brought back to me at the hospital. I was so upset when I saw those glasses. They should have been broken, shattered in a million pieces. My kids were, our little dog Minnie, all three of them killed in that tent that day.

Why in hell did God leave me here but take them? It was a question I asked myself all the time. I wanted to know where I was supposed to go and what kind of person I was supposed to be now. I was so bitter. I hated God for taking them from me yet making me stay here to live without them. I was a sad, lonely child who had a horrible hard life. I couldn't believe my adult life was going to be a hard one either. I wondered what I had done as a child and into my adulthood to have deserved any of what life had dished me. Grieving is so hard they say there are many different stages of grief.

There isn't a day that's gone by when I don't think about my kids. What might they look and sound like, and what are their likes and dislikes? Would they be sassy pants or rule followers? They were beautiful and perfect, and I had created them and kept them safe for forty weeks, and then one day, in the blink of an eye, they were gone. Never to be spoken about in front of people, in fear of someone getting emotional and causing a river of feelings to emerge. I didn't want anyone to know my true feelings. I wanted everyone to know I was good, on the mend, feeling good about life now.

I have videos I will occasionally pull out and look at. Dustin had some speech issues and was in a speech at his preschool. When I started watching the videos, it had been a while since the accident. I realized I couldn't understand what he was saying. I was so upset that I had forgotten what his words sounded like. I had forgotten how to make out his words because I wasn't with him daily. Noticing that small, what should have been an insignificant piece to my puzzle made me cry and scream inside. I didn't mean to forget what his voice sounded like, but I had, and it was unbearably difficult to get past. They had been gone too long at this point, and I was still stuck in that time frame. Most of the time, my memories of them were of the accident and the last moments I had with them.

Now year four was a whole new pain level for me. Year four after losing my kids, I received a devastating call. A call that essentially broke me the rest of the way.

"We're looking for a Mrs. Callie Palet," the caller said.

"You've reached her. What can I do for you?"

"Ma'am, I'm sorry to bother you, but we need you to come down to the hospital. It's regarding your husband, Jake."

"Jake, is he okay? What's wrong with him?"

"Ma'am, I can't really answer any questions over the phone. Could you come down here as soon as you can?"

"I'm on my way, sir. I'll be there in fifteen minutes. What floor do I go to?"

"I'll meet you at the entrance, ma'am. I'll be waiting there for your arrival."

Thoughts flooded me like a raging bull. I knew Jake was hurting, and I also knew Jake hadn't been acting himself that morning before he left for work. But I never ever thought what was in store for me at that hospital would have been something I was walking into. Everything moved in slow motion after arriving. The police officer shook my hand and asked me to follow him somewhere private so that we could talk.

"Okay, but can I see Jake first, please? What's this about, officer?"

"I'm so sorry, ma'am. I will answer your questions, but please do follow me first."

I wish I had turned around and left the hospital to effectively restart that day over, hugged Jake one more time, and told him I loved him. I wish for once that I was enough for one person to want to live, that I was enough for someone to fight for their life. But I wasn't.

That officer broke me that day the rest of the way. He told me that my Jake had been found hanging in his office by three ties from the ceiling fan. There was a suicide note address to me. He suffered so much after losing the kids, and I sat back and did nothing to help. Don't get me wrong. I tried to pull Jake out of the hole he fell in, and I tried to bring him back to the light, but he was too far gone by the time I noticed something was wrong.

"I wasn't enough for him to fight for his life, Nate. Our life just wasn't enough. He stated that in the letter he left for me. He left me a goddamn letter telling me I was his gem," I laughed and continued, "a fucking letter telling me I wasn't enough to keep him here. To move on and find someone worthy. Who the hell does shit like that, Nate, huh? I'll tell you who, Nate, it was one of the most amazing men I'd ever laid eyes on, that's who. He was my other half, the ying to my yang. My soulmate and I broke him. I left him alone to suffer in his own grief while I was busy drinking my life and grief away. If I had spent time helping Jake cope, he would have lived, you know?"

"Or, Callie, maybe he wouldn't have," Nate said.

"You promised not to talk until I was finished."

"Right," he said and zipped his mouth again.

"When I buried Jake, I buried Callie that day as well. The beautiful, happy, loving Callie died the day Jake took his life, and in her place was this scared, cowardly, lonely widow. I kept all his clothes and locked myself in this house. Refused to talk to my friends and family. Hell, I only have one friend left, and I don't judge them. They left because I wouldn't let them in. I never answered their calls or the door when they showed up. Layla is the only one who continued to still bother with me. She actually sat out on my porch in the twenty-degree weather until I would answer my door to her. She stayed out there for two and a half hours talking to me, well, herself, really since I was ignoring her on the other side of the door. I don't know who I am without Jake. He died two years ago now, and still

I grabbed my shirt and pulled it out a bit to put emphasis on it. I wear his T-shirts to bed. I keep his favorite ice cream on hand even though I hate it. I talk to him even though he's dead, Nate, and get no response back, so I guess that's a good sign." I tried to throw a tiny joke, even though it was not funny in the least.

"I can't let myself be happy, don't you see, Nate? I didn't, couldn't save any of them. They all died, and I stood back and watched it happen. I was helpless. Nothing I could have done would have saved them. I know that realistically. But my head and heart scream, 'You lived, and they didn't. You're a terrible mother and wife. Why didn't you try harder to find a solution? A better doctor, something!' Instead, I stayed here, barely surviving, waiting for the day I was called home or wherever my afterlife would be.

"So you see, Nate, I'm a coward who hides downstairs in my bathtub whenever it rains, no matter the amount or kind. I have panic attacks occasionally, and I'm broken. A sad excuse for a woman, but I'm me, nonetheless, and that's all I have. I do my job, and I do it great because I have to live to be punished for living and them dying. I deserve to be lonely, crazy, and unloved. I deserve to be hated. I didn't protect them. I didn't save them because I didn't know how. I was supposed to figure out a way, and I failed. I really don't know, but that's my past story, and now you know who Jake, Dustin, and Savannah are.

"So am I fired? Do you want to find someone more put together, someone who won't have to take the rainy days off because she can't leave her house in fear she'll freak out and cause a scene? Now's your chance to end this business deal and walk out of here, Nate. I won't hate you or even blame you if you do. I never meant for you to see me that way, nor did I want you to hear this story, but now you have, and that's all there is to me. Heartbreak and sadness, so you can't do any more damage to me than what's already been done, Nate. Now's your turn to make a decision."

Chapter 15

Callie

"Well, are you going to say anything, Nate?"

"Oh, is it my turn now?" he said with a smirk.

"If you have anything to say, yes, Nate, it is."

"Okay, so first, that's a lot, Callie. I know you said not to say it, but I really am so sorry that happened to you."

I opened my mouth to say something, and a finger pushed on my lips.

"Shh, not yet let me finish. Why do you feel like you're unworthy of love? If it's because of your husband Jake taking his life, I can assure you that his life with you won't be forgotten because you find someone who makes you happy again. You weren't at fault for anything in that story. I know my words aren't helping, but I guess I don't understand the kind of loss you've experienced, so I'm not quite getting your feelings on the situation. I could not imagine losing a child. That kind of pain has got to be unbearable, and for that, I am truly sorry, but you are worthy, and it sounds like you loved them very much. I'm sure you were a fantastic mother to them. I couldn't tell you what your husband was thinking when he wrote you that letter nor took his life, leaving you alone in a time when you needed him as well. You are only one person. How can you expect yourself to take care of someone else when nobody is helping you take care of you? When was the last time you actually did something for you? Something that made you feel good, like getting a massage or a pedicure. I know women like those. Can I ask something of you, Callie?"

I was blinking so rapidly to try to hold the tears that I just bit my lower lip and shook my head yes.

"Can I hug you? I promise I'm not pitying you. I genuinely feel like you need a hug right now."

I burst into tears, shaking my head yes while he wrapped his arms around me, one hand holding my lower back, pulling me to him and the other rubbing the back of my hair down like a parent would console their child.

"That's it. Let it out. Sometimes, crying is good for you. My mom always said crying cleanses the soul."

I cried harder at that. He even has smart parents. I gripped his shoulders with each hand wrapped around and under his arms.

"I'm sorry I'm such a blubbering mess," I managed to get out in between tears.

"It's okay. I still think you're absolutely beautiful, Callie."

I blushed and put my head back on his shoulder when he put his finger under my chin, raised my head, and whispered, "I'm going to kiss you, Callie. If you don't want me to, now would be the time to say so." He waited a few moments, searching my eyes before our lips locked.

It's like fireworks on the Fourth of July were exploding all around us, and we were in a battle to reach the finish line, both of us trying to take the lead. It has been so long since I had kissed anyone. I never felt anything like this. Jake and I were soft and gentle with each other. What is this? Passion, fiery, needy, and, oh my god, so good? I was the first to break away, panting and needing air.

"That was—"

"Amazing!" Nate interrupted me.

"I was going to say fan-fucking-tastic, but amazing will do. You and I are about to start working together though, Nate, and I'm pretty messed up. I'm not sure we should do that again."

"What are you saying right now, Callie? That was the best kiss of my life, and I'm not exaggerating!"

"Please, I'm not stupid, Nate. I have only ever kissed my husband, so I know I'm not that good at kissing."

"Why do you always talk down on yourself? Your kiss blew me away, and that is the truth. You looked stunning tonight. I wanted to go to the bar and pluck out the drunk's eyes that kept looking at you tonight at Mila's. You're so oblivious to your own beauty. You really have no idea how attractive you are, do you?"

"I'm not that nice-looking," I said while rolling my eyes.

"No, Callie, I'm serious. You are hands down one of the most beautiful women I've ever laid eyes on, and the fact that you don't see that kills me. We may have just met, but I want to help you. You make me want to save you. You are worth fixing, not that you're broken, but fixing in the sense of seeing what others around you see and think of you. Understanding that the traumas you experienced with losing your children and Jake's death are things that were beyond your control. There is nothing you could have done that would have changed the outcome of either day. You are not responsible for someone else's mental health. You can try getting them help, showing them compassion and tough love when they need it. I'm sure there are things you could have done differently, but it wouldn't have changed anything. You can hate me if you want, but what Jake did was wrong. I understand he was grieving for his children, but he forgot about you. He forgot that you were a part of his life also and that he was breaking you down by writing that letter. You are enough, Callie, and I'd love to show you how much I'd like to fight for you by giving you some numbers of therapists my sister used to overcome her traumas. I can't talk you through it, but I can get you someone who can."

"Nate, I have talked to people, and it doesn't help trust me."

"Just take them, Callie. Look them up, read their reviews, find out their strengths and specialty, and choose one who will benefit you. It's all at your fingertips right now, okay? I'm offering it free of charge, all on me, just take it and get better. Do it for you, for your happiness and peace of mind. Even if you don't want to go on a date with me, it's still an offer I'm leaving out there for you, okay? I'm going to go now before I kiss you again but think about it. Here, Braxton Long, 332-555-6578."

Nate leaned down and kissed my cheek, saying softly in my ear, "Have a great rest of your evening, beautiful, and I'll be in touch."

    Watching Nate leave my house, I reached up and touched my lips with my fingers, wondering what the hell just happened. Nate kissed me and told me I was not crazy or fired after hearing my entire story. How is it possible he doesn't hate me? I have thought since the day of the accident that everything that happened to the kids, to Jake and me, was my fault. I hadn't put enough effort into those around me or paid enough attention to see the tragic truth that Jake was lost and suicidal. Maybe I should look this guy up and do a search and see if he will benefit me. The worst thing that can happen is it does nothing, like the others I tried after the accident.

    I set the card to the side, got up to clean the dishes from our tea, and started shutting down the lights for the night, exhausted.

Chapter 16

Callie

Waking to my phone ringing, I groaned, rolling over, ready to tell off whoever the hell is disturbing my sleep to see it's a message from Nate. He must have programmed his number into my phone last night at some point.

"Good morning. I hope you had a great night's sleep. I was hoping to meet up for lunch today if you are available."

I don't know what to do. Should I be embarrassed over my behavior last night and turn down the lunch? On the other hand, that kiss we shared was so electric. Should I pursue this and see where it leads? I really am confused. I always promised I wouldn't ever date again. Is that a promise I should hold up to? I don't want to cheat on Jake. I know he's gone, and I shouldn't feel this way, but I do. Maybe we'll take baby steps and see where it leads. I think that's the best I can offer at this point.

"Good morning to you as well, Nate. I did sleep well, thank you for asking. Unfortunately, I have prior lunch plans, but rain check?"

I hope Layla can meet for lunch. I don't mean to lie to Nate. I just need to process everything that happened and talk about it with someone else. I know Layla will tell me I'm over thinking, but I feel scared.

This is so new and out of the norm for me to even be attracted to someone else. What if it's just my hormones being crazy and next week, I'll regret everything?

My thoughts consumed me, and I felt so shitty just thinking about letting Nate kiss me. What would Jake think of me now? Does it even matter the other part of my brain is screaming? Jake is gone, I tell myself, you've done nothing wrong. Breathe, Callie, everything is fine.

I got up and took an Ativan since I was already on the verge of a panic attack, and it was not even raining. After showering and getting dressed, I went into the living room, turned on the morning news channel, and started my coffee. First sip in, and I heard my doorbell ring. Who the hell could be here? I wasn't expecting anyone.

"Mrs. Callie Palet?" I heard when I opened the door.

"Yes, this is she," I said.

"Here you go, ma'am. Someone sure wanted to please you," he said and handed me two dozen flowers. The first bouquet of flowers was a rose mix with red, white, and pink roses. They smelled divine, and I love roses. The second was a mixture of lilies, daisies, and some sunflowers. I saw there was a card attached to both, so I carefully put them on my table and plucked the card from both bouquets. The card from the daisies, lilies, and sunflowers read:

> Dear Mrs. Palet,
>
> Please accept my dearest and sincerest apologies for knocking you down with my door.
>
> Sincerely,
> Nate Owens

The second card from the roses I opened next:

> Sweet Callie,
>
> I hope you enjoyed our night as much as I did. I hope you know there is a lot more to me than what you see on the outside as well. We all have our pasts, and we all have a future. I sincerely hope that you are in my future. From a man waiting for another date.
>
> Nate

Oh my! What have I gotten myself into? This man is making me hot, and he's not even in the same room. I fanned myself with the card, contemplating if I should text him and thank him for the flowers. I guess that would be fine, but I'd wait until after lunch, which reminded me to shoot Layla a message asking about lunch. After receiving a "Hell yes, girl" from Layla, I went in search of something to wear, settling on some holy jeans and an off-the-shoulder thin sweater. I grabbed my water and headed out to meet Layla.

Arriving first, of course, since Layla was always fashionably late, I grabbed what used to be my favorite table in the back corner, looking out so I could see what was happening in the world. We decided on this little mom-and-pop shop called the Tater Shop. It has the best chicken salad ever and the most delectable muffins. Waiting for Layla, I decided to search for this therapist that Nate gave me. I would love to be the person I used to be if that is remotely possible. I have to remind myself not to get my hopes up that nothing has worked in the past. Finally, I saw Layla walking up, so I waved to her.

"Girl, a person would starve waiting on you." I laughed as Layla stuck her tongue out at me and grabbed me for a hug.

"I can't wait to hear all about last night, Callie Marie!" she said.

I started rehashing my terrible start to my night all the way to the juicy kiss and him leaving me with numbers of therapists, the text, flowers, all of it.

Chapter 17

Callie

"Gosh, girl, leave it to you to find a romantic man while I'm over here struggling like 'Hey! Over here, boys!'"

I laughed at that and gave her a gentle shove on her shoulder. "You are so beautiful, Layla. Your match is out there. Let him come to you."

We decided after lunch to take a stroll through the park and down the landing to the water. Layla stopped walking, and I stopped after realizing she was not right next to me anymore. When I turned around, I got wrapped in a hug I was not expecting.

"Hey," I said, hugging her back, "what was that for, Layla?"

"That's the first time I've seen my best friend in a really long time, and it felt really good to see you in there."

"Yeah, I'm sorry I've been such a shitty friend to you, Layla. You didn't deserve any of what I threw at you. I'm surprised you didn't walk away and never look back."

"I already told you, you're stuck with me forever, no matter what. Now can we please, girl, talk some more?"

"Oh, you and your girl talk, Layla, I swear." I laughed. "What do you have in mind to talk about Layla?"

"Oh, you know, just you and lover boy and the next date. You're going to say yes to a date, right, Callie?"

"You really think I should, Layla? You think I have enough to offer a man like Nate Owens?"

"Are you kidding me, Callie Marie Palet? Look at you. You're model material with your beautiful eyes and long legs. You are just as worthy of him, and he should be thankful to even have someone like you in his arms. Of course, you have plenty to offer someone like him. You may be innocent and all, but I guarantee that man can teach you some things, girl," she said, and I knew my face was as red as a tomato.

"I am not that innocent, Layla."

"Really? So you and Jake were freaks in the sheets then, huh?"

"What? Oh my god, Layla, stop it! You can't seriously want details like that."

"See, that's my point. You don't see me getting all red in the face at the mention of sex, Callie."

"Maybe I'm just a private person, Layla," I said while raising one eyebrow.

"Okay, so answer me this: what colors are your vibrator?"

"What the hell, Layla? We are in public in a park, for god's sake. There are children here!"

"You don't have one, do you, Callie?"

Looking around to make sure nobody has heard the absurd conversation she is insisting on having with me, I answered quickly, "No. Now can we please move on from this conversation?"

"Mmmm-hmmm, exactly what I thought, Mrs. Innocent Pants. I will let you out of this convo for now, but only to come back to it another time. So seriously, I wonder if Mr. Sexy Pants has a friend," Layla said while raising her eyebrows up and down.

"I have no idea actually, Layla."

"Well, too bad my perfect man wouldn't just drop from the heavens right in front of me." Layla laughed with praying hands.

"Layla, if you wouldn't be so picky, you'd have a man, you know? You remember Tate? He was head over heels for you, if I remember correctly. Even went as far as to buy you a ring, and you were quick to stop that relationship, letting him know it just wasn't the right feel for you. I believe you said, 'You have qualities I like, but I just don't feel like you're my forever.' I'd never actually seen a man so distraught and lost. He must have called and texted you fifty times in a span of a week, begging you to just give him a chance that he could change what you didn't like."

"Ya, he was a sweetie but not assertive or dominant enough for me, Callie." Layla laughed. "I actually felt bad that I didn't feel the same way. I did try, Callie, for a full year trying to make myself love him with my whole heart. I did love him, just not enough to commit to a married everyday life with him. I heard he found someone who makes him very happy from a mutual friend, so that's good. I know my perfect man is out there, just waiting for me to find him. Problem is I'm tired of waiting. For now, I'll just live vicariously through you, my dear bestest friend. I'm growing cobwebs. It's been so long since I've had a man." She laughed. "Do me a favor, Callie, and let that man satisfy you so one of us is at least getting some!"

Layla laughed so hard at the look on my face.

"Ya, I don't think so, Layla, not anytime soon anyway. I'm barely ready to talk to society, let alone let someone intimately touch me." I laughed and gave Layla a shoulder bump with mine.

"Well, it was worth asking." Layla laughed. "Also, I have to get back to work. Love you, girl, and text that man back ASAP. Let me know when. I have the perfect dress for the next date. It's my newest design, and it's not even been released yet, so feel special, girl. You know I'd never do this for anyone."

"I know you wouldn't. Thank you from the bottom of my heart. Now get to work. I'll text you."

Chapter 18

Callie

Sitting on a bench watching the water after Layla left, I found myself wondering how I got to this place. I felt like I was healing a little bit maybe. I felt so much more myself the last week, even letting Layla in more. I'm not sure what has changed, but maybe now would be the perfect time to set up a meeting with Mr. Long and see if he can help me. I grabbed my phone and dialed his number before I talked myself out of it.

"Hello, Braxton Long's office. How can I help you?"

"Hello, my name's Callie Palet, and I was given Mr. Long's number by a friend and was wondering if he has any openings anytime soon?"

"Ahh, Mrs. Palet, yes, Braxton told me if you call to schedule you right away."

"Oh, he did?"

"How about today at two?"

"Today? Umm, I, I'm not sure of my schedule. I, uh, okay, I guess I can do that." If I'm going to try, I guess I should jump right into it. I hung up and felt a tear fall. I wanted to feel happy again. I'd give anything to be just a smidge happy and normal. I've been hiding inside myself for so long. I'm not sure I even know who I am or how to be me again. I'm scared to release any of the feelings I keep bottled up, in fear that it'll take me back to severely depressed Callie. The thoughts I used to have were scary at times, and it bothered me to think that was me at one point. Here goes nothing, I guess.

By the time I got to my car and got going, I should arrive right on time.

"Good afternoon, ma'am. I'm Callie Palet here to see Mr. Long."

"Yes, yes, right this way, hon. You want anything to drink? We have water, tea, or coffee."

"Uh, no thanks, I'm good for now."

"Absolutely. Let me know if you need anything."

"Thank you, I will."

"Have a seat in here. Braxton will be in soon."

I shook my head at her as I began to get nervous. At this point, my leg was bouncing up and down. I was drumming my fingers on my knee with one hand, and the other was in my mouth, chewing on my nails. I should just go. I don't think I'm ready for this. It's not going to help. I got up to the door when I heard a knock.

"Come in," I said with a small squeaky voice.

"Good afternoon, Callie. I'm so sorry to have kept you waiting. I had a few notes to finish on my last client. Please have a seat, and let's get to know each other a little bit."

I sat on the couch, and he sat across from me.

"Hello, Callie. Is it okay that I call you by your first name?"

I shook my head yes and said, "That's fine. I actually prefer it."

"Perfect! Well, I'm Braxton Long. You may call me Braxton as well. Anything you'd like to know about me, Callie?"

"I'm not really sure, Mr. Long."

"Please, Callie, call me Braxton. I can tell you're nervous, and that's okay, but let me reassure you that today, we just get to know each other a little bit. No talking about your situation unless you want to or why you were sent to me or chose to see me, okay? So I'll just tell you a little bit, and you can ask questions if you have any in between, okay?"

"All right." I shook my head. "Sounds fair."

"So I've told you my name. Now let me tell you a bit about me, okay? Let's see, I'm a dog person. I don't hate cats, but given the choice, I'd choose a dog any day. You met my wife out front. Amazing woman that one. She's quite the pistol when she's angry but loves with her whole heart," he said while giving a small laugh. I found myself giving a small giggle as well at that.

Okay, I'm relaxing a bit. This is okay. I can do this.

"We have four kids, all grown except for the surprise baby. She's seventeen for a few more months anyway. Let me see what else I could tell you, hmm…" he said. "Any questions yet, Callie?"

I shook my head. "Sorry, none yet."

"All right, well, why I'm thinking of something more to share about me, how about you tell me a bit about yourself if that's all right with you?"

"Well, you know my name. I'm an interior decorator, and I love my job. It's fantastic to take something bland and make it vibrant and alive again. I love cats and dogs but don't have any since they require attention, and I don't have much to give these days. My son loved all animals. I used to think he'd be a veterinarian or something because he was so into them."

"You have children then, I take it."

"Used to," I said while wringing my fingers together.

"I'm sorry about your loss. That must be so hard. How old were they, if I may ask?"

I looked up at him and decided I liked him. He's got kind eyes, and he's not pushing or telling me what I should be doing like the others used to straight off the bat.

"My son was four and my daughter nine months when they died."

He shook his head. "If it's okay with you, I'd like to hear more about your children."

"What do you want to know?"

"Anything you want to share about them with me."

"Okay, I'll try this," I said to myself. "I guess we can start with my son. His name was Dustin, and he had brown hair and brown eyes, and he was a major spitfire. He was a loving kid who loved bug juice and his blankets. Man, his blankets. He would fight others if they even tried to use his blanket or share it with him. That was a huge no in his book. Those were just his, and nobody else was allowed to use them. His favorite cartoon was Go, Diego, Go. He had just started to learn to pedal his bike. Once, my sister and I took him out for a bike ride in our neighborhood. We were riding and talking when he decided to pull his bike in front of someone's yard and say it ran out of power. I laughed so hard. There was a man in his yard who agreed with him, saying he had seen it happen when it ran out of power. He was a great kid, and I miss him terribly," I said while grabbing the tissue from Braxton to wipe my eyes.

"He sounds like a great kid."

"Was a great kid."

"Callie, just because he's not here anymore doesn't mean he isn't still a great kid. He existed. He was a huge part of your life, and he's still a big part of your heart, right?"

I shook my head yes while a loud sob burst from my body.

"It's going to be okay. You can still love him, Callie. He's a part of you whether he is here or on the other side. It's okay to want him still. It's okay to feel sad, angry, confused. All of those emotions are normal. Losing a child is the worst pain. I've never lost one before, but I can tell you from my experience as a therapist that parents who have lost a child are the hardest on themselves. The pain from losing their child eats at them until it completely consumes them. I've met only a select few who have fought their way back and gone on to be happy again. Some parents can't deal with the loss of their child, and that's where I aim to perfect. I want to help you understand your loss and get you back to a happy baseline or as happy as you'll let yourself be. Tell me about your daughter. You said she was nine months?"

Tears were falling like a fountain. I'd tell him a few details about my baby. "Her name was Savannah. She was beautiful with brown hair like her brother's, brown eyes, and perfect size. She wasn't chunky, but not thin either, just right in between the two. She had learned to play patty cake right before the accident. Just started to pull herself up in her bed and playpen. Her laugh was so sweet and contagious. The night before the accident, she was laughing so hard in a way I'd never seen her do before. I would sit up and say 'boo,' and she'd laugh so hysterically. I must have played that game with her for half an hour before she grew tired of it. I miss them so much, Braxton. There are days I beg for it to be my time just so I can hold them again. I need to hold them again. Some days, it takes all the energy I have just to get up and use the bathroom. Those are the days that I'm locked inside in my own head, and I can't focus. Everything around me becomes a blur, and the only thing playing are my memories over and over and over again. It's a cycle I can't seem to stop."

I'm an ugly crier, and my face gets all red and blotchy, but I really don't care right now. I'm sure I'm not the only person who looks like this in his line of work.

"The fact that you can tell me about them and release some bound-up feelings tells me that you've already started to mend your heart. You know what is healthy and unhealthy, and you force yourself to face it head-on if I'm correct in hearing the little bit I have. I believe we can work through this together and get you to who you will become without your children with you. If you're willing, I think we could set something up maybe twice a month."

"I think I can do that."

"Good, I think this was a great start to our sessions. I'm looking forward to getting to know you a bit better."

"Thank you, but aren't you going to tell me what I should do before our next session?"

"No, should I be giving you things to work on?"

"I don't know. The other therapists always did."

"Callie, you already did the work today. You've opened up on your own. I didn't need to push you or even ask you more than once to tell me about them. You did that on your own free will, and that was your only job today. Now schedule with Mary Jo for two weeks, okay? It was very nice to meet you."

Chapter 19

Nate

Leaving Callie after she had just told me that horrific story that was her life was the last thing I wanted to do. I knew kissing her while she was so vulnerable was wrong, but I had to show her that she was desirable and that I wanted her. She needed to know that just because her husband chose to leave her in the worst way possible that it wasn't her fault. I am so pissed at the man, and if ever given the chance, I'd probably deck his ass just for the tears she lost over him and his selfish words he wrote to her. You want to take your life, fine, but to tell her that her love wasn't enough to keep him here, what the hell was that? I knew if I didn't get out of there soon, I'd be attempting to take her right where she sat. When she came out in that baggy shirt, I knew it was a man's, but she still looked delectable. I almost touched her face on instinct but caught myself, not sure what she would do, and I did not want to push it at that moment. I thought for sure she was going to kiss me at one point when she was leaning in, only for her to ask me to sit.

Listening to her story was hard. That is so much loss for one person. I understand now why she is guarded. Guessing I'd be scared to lose anyone close to me also if I were in her shoes. I wasn't lying when I told her that was the best kiss of my life. I had never experienced something that great before. It was as if she was meant to only be kissing me. All I knew when she broke that kiss was I wanted more, more kisses, more of her. Keeping control of myself was so hard when my body was reacting to the kiss in such a way that I thought my button might pop off my pants with how hard I was.

I was serious when I told her she would have any specialist at her reach free of charge, even if she didn't want anything to do with me after that. She can't see what the rest of the world sees, and I can't help but put some of that blame on her late husband. How could he not treat her as if she were his everything? I know I've never lost children before, but I couldn't imagine not putting that woman first.

I took an extremely cold shower when I got home to try to tame my friend since he was still saluting after sharing that very intimate kiss with Callie. I wasn't sure it'd ever go down. Waking in the morning, I called the flower shop to order some roses, just to show her that I was thinking about her, and threw out a few words for the card.

They were set to deliver flowers to her any way that Gretchen had ordered after I knocked her down. I had no idea what Gretchen wrote on the card of that bouquet, but it didn't really matter. I shot her a quick text, hoping she'd have lunch with me today, only to receive a no but raincheck. I'm hoping that she will reach back out and let me show her how much I would fight for her and treat her like the queen she deserves to be treated as.

I shot Lincoln a text asking if he could meet me for lunch and a couple of beers. I need to hash this shit out with someone before I explode, and he is my best friend. Jumping in the shower, I quickly shot a message to Gretchen to cancel my appointments for the day, saying that I had something come up, so I'd be back tomorrow.

Lincoln and I pulled up to my favorite pub, Brewski Lounge, and ordered our lunch and a couple of beers.

"All right, what's up, Nate? You never take off work unless it's something serious, so what happened that we are out during the day having beers and skipping work?"

"Nothing really. It's just this girl I told you about, the one we hired to do the renovation, Lincoln. She is so lost and had a bunch of bad shit happen to her. I want to help her, Linc, but I don't know how. She won't let me in."

"You really have it bad for this girl, don't ya, Nate? I told you to just get laid, didn't I? It usually cures any issue that is girl-related."

"I don't know, Linc. This chick is special. I can feel it in my bones, and my body is saying find a way to keep her that I need her."

"Wow, bro, you really do have it bad."

"I kissed her last night, and I shouldn't have because it could have backfired, and I would have been taking advantage of her, but I swear that wasn't my intention, man. I just felt so strongly she needed to know that others do desire her and that I was willing to fight for her if she would let me. But the kiss, Lincoln, god, the kiss was the best damn kiss of my life, dude. I'm not even sure I could kiss another chick after having that one. It was as if we were the only two people in the universe, and it was set up just for us and us alone, that we were always destined to meet and share that intimate kiss. Do you know what I mean?"

"No, Nate." He laughed. "I've never felt attached to a woman besides a friend-with-benefit kind of thing."

"I don't know what to do, Lincoln. I'm serious. I want to be in this woman's life."

"Then woo her, my dude. Let her see the best sides of you. Be persistent but not pushy. Ask her what she wants. Tell her what you want and let her know exactly what you just told me. If she hangs the moon and stars for you, then don't let her slip away."

"I asked her to lunch today, and she turned me down, telling me raincheck. I thought for sure she felt what I did when we kissed, especially since she called it fan-fucking-tastic, but it wasn't enough to make her want more from me."

"Well, you did say she's been through some shit, Nate. Do you think maybe she's scared to get close to anyone else or some shit?"

"No, I guess I didn't think of it that way. I'll wait and see if she responds to me later before I send her another text. Let's get out of here and go play some basketball, yeah?"

"Sure, I guess I could play a bit, but I can't promise I'll let you win this time."

"Yeah, right, bro, you've never let me win. Don't even act like that." He laughed.

"You're such a sore loser, Lincoln."

Chapter 20

Callie

Leaving Braxton's office, I felt better than I had in a long time. I decided to go for a drive after leaving, going nowhere in particular, just driving and thinking over every single detail in my life. Mostly about Nate and the feelings I had for him that were building.

I think I'm going to accept his offer for a date. One date can't hurt anything, and if it feels off, I won't do it again. It feels good to be decisive and not overthink everything. I feel a bit more in control of my life than usual. Braxton didn't really do anything. All he did was listen and tell me a few things, but it felt different. Like he was actually understanding me and my thoughts and emotions. I finally backed into my driveway and decided to soak in my tub. I put my favorite peachy bliss bubble bath in, turned it on hot, and started lighting a few candles to help me relax. I grabbed a bottle of white wine and hurried back to check my tub, undressing and slipping into a robe while I waited for the tub to finish filling. While I waited, I grabbed my phone and sent Nate a message.

"Good evening, Nate. After a long day, you're still on my mind. So I decided I would very much like to take you up on your offer for a real date. If you still want to, that is fine."

I read it before I sent it and decided those weren't the right words, so I deleted them and started over.

"Hi, Nate. After a very productive day and my mind being preoccupied with thoughts of you, I've decided I would very much like to go on a date with you. When is a good day and time for you?"

There. I sent it, and I can't even begin to tell you how scared and nervous I am. What if he changed his mind after I blew him off or he found out I really didn't have a prior lunch? I quickly shut my thoughts down, turned the faucet off, climbed into my bath, and just soaked down. Let my feelings and emotions go for the time being and focus on how I feel right at this moment in this amazing-smelling bath with my wine and candles lit. I heard my phone vibrate, so I leaned up, took a sip of my wine, dried my hand, and picked it up.

"Hey, beautiful, I was hoping you'd reach out and want to go on a date with me. You pick the day and time, and I'll do the rest. I want you to feel special. Just so you know, I will be doing plenty of wooing for you on this date, so expect big."

Wooing, huh? I don't even know what the hell wooing is. I laughed. *Layla will be so proud of me*, I thought with a sigh. I quickly responded back.

"I don't expect big. My expectations are somewhat low, considering I think I've only really been on one date, so the bar isn't set very high. Please don't feel the need to go above and beyond."

I finished my first glass of wine and refilled my glass. *One more won't hurt*, I said to myself.

"Well, that makes me want to make it even more special so that you understand nobody can outdo my date with you. I plan to be the most romantic gentleman, my lady."

I giggled at that and set my phone down, trying to decide what I wanted to respond with. He is so sexy I can envision him smirking at me right now. I must have been thinking too long because now I was two glasses down, borderline drunk, and poured myself another glass when my phone rang.

Looking, I realized it was Nate. Why would he be calling? I thought we were texting.

"Hello?"

"Hey, Callie, I'm sorry if I was being too much."

"Uh, what are you talking about, Nate?"

"Well, you left me on read."

"Oh." I laughed. "I was thinking about what to write back."

I heard his laugh rumble through the phone. "You are so sexy, Nate Owens." I didn't realize I had said it out loud, but I guess I did because his laughter stopped.

"Oh really, beautiful, tell me more."

I knew my face was super red, and I was blushing.

"I have no idea what you're talking about."

"Mmhmm, sure you don't, 'you are so sexy, Nate Owens,'" he mocked me.

"Oh my gosh, shut up." I laughed. Maybe I had one too many glasses of wine while I soaked in my tub.

"Do tell me more, madam, the tub, huh? I bet it's lonely in that tub with just you."

"It happens to be just fine, thank you."

"Well, I'm officially jealous of water and your bathtub. I'll let you go so you can finish your relaxation, but don't forget to shoot me a day and time, okay, beautiful?"

"All right, Nate, I will. I'm excited to go on this date with you." God, I sound so childish, but I can't help it. I really am excited; I haven't felt this alive in a really long time.

"Dido, babe, I'm glad you accepted my offer for a date. See you soon, okay?"

I took a breath and sighed, then squealed and kicked my feet a bit, but not too much that the water splashed out. I finished my bath and decided to call Layla to find out what day was okay for her to help me get ready.

"Hey, Layla, how are you?"

"Enough with the formalities, girl. What's up?"

"Well, I may have messaged Nate and taken him up on his offer for a real date." I had to pull the phone away from my ear. Layla screamed so loudly.

"I am so proud of you, Callie Marie! It's about damn time you do something to make yourself happy. Now what can I do to help?"

"Well, I was hoping you'd still lend me that dress and help me get ready."

"Of course, that's a no-brainer, Callie. I wouldn't miss this day for anything. When is the date?"

"I haven't scheduled a day yet. I wanted to check with you and see when you were off to help me."

"Girl, tell him tomorrow before you overthink this and take it back." She laughed. She's right though. I do tend to overthink things and then go backward.

"Okay, I'll see you tomorrow, Layla, and thank you again!"

"No problem! This is what friends are for!"

Okay, now to message Nate.

"So…is tomorrow night too soon for our date?"

I'm so tipsy right now I find myself giggling at the thought of me having a date with this amazing man who I really don't even know anything about besides he owns this huge corporation. I suppose that's what dates are for.

Hearing my phone beep, I quickly grabbed it, knowing it was a message from Nate.

"Tomorrow, huh? You really are testing me, aren't you, beautiful? I believe that's ample enough time for me to pull something special off for you. How about 5:00 p.m.?"

Layla didn't specify a time, so I guess five it'll be.

"Five p.m. will be great, Mr. Sexy Hazel Eyes."

I decided to be a bit flirty. At least, I think it's flirty. I'm not really sure. I've been out of service for so long.

"You like my eyes, beautiful? I happen to think every part of you is sexy, Callie Palet, and I look forward to showing you tomorrow evening. Have a great rest of your night, and I'll see you tomorrow, okay?"

I'm blushing so hard right now, and nobody is even here to see or hear anything we're saying to each other, but I can't seem to help it.

"You too! See you tomorrow."

Now to just keep myself thinking positive things so I don't get all into my head about things, I sighed and shut down the lights, climbing into bed and praying for happy dreams of Nate and not of my beloved ones I can't reach anymore.

Chapter 21

Nate

In the middle of a game of basketball with Lincoln, my phone pinged, so I took a time out, grabbed my water, drinking half of it in one go, and grabbed my phone. I told Lincoln I forfeited after seeing the message Callie just sent me.

"She wants to go on a date, Lincoln," I said. Linc slapped my shoulder.

"I knew she would, man! Now the balls in your court, Nate. Show her why she should choose you."

"She's in the tub. Holy bloody hell, this girl is going to kill me." It took everything I had not to drive to her house so she could see how sexy I could be. I didn't know how much she had to drink, so I grounded myself to my spot and just flirted a bit with her. I don't know yet where or what I'm going to do for this date, but I need to make it good. To the point and very special. Over the top special.

"Lincoln, I've got to go, dude. I got plans to make. You good, or you want me to have George drop you somewhere?"

"Nah, dude. I'm good. You go ahead, win your girl."

I got almost home and got a message saying 5:00 p.m. was perfect, so I quickly teased her a little and got to making those plans since I didn't have very much time to pull it all together. I called the floral department store and asked for as many roses as they had on hand or, better yet, just the petals. Made a list of everything I needed so I could head to the store and get it all before I headed to the spot to set it up for her. Of course, everybody and their brother is at the damn store, and I can't just be rude and ignore them. Shit, I groaned, maybe just put my head down and pretend I don't see her. I think to myself as I see my stepmom's best friend coming up the aisle in front of me.

"Nate, is that you?" I heard and I swear I wanted to just pluck my ears off and pretend they didn't work.

"Hello, Sicily, how are you?"

"Oh, I'm great," she said with a smile. "Just shopping for my mom, you know, since she's only getting older. I swear she's losing it these days, always putting stuff in the wrong spot, and I have to look for it when I need it," she said.

I thought, *No, it's probably where she likes it to be, not where you think it should be placed.* "Oh well, that's definitely not good," I said.

"No, it's definitely not. I may have to start looking into assisted living for her soon if it continues," she said.

I swear I can't stand this lady, and why my stepmom is best friends with her is beyond me because she's all sweet and kind, while Sicily is all stuck up, rude, and selfish. She only ever thinks of herself. If she didn't stop this nonsense small talk soon, I was sure to lose my temper with her ignorance and awful comments about the person who brought her into this world and cared for her until she could take over for herself. A person should always respect their parents.

Sicily, completely unaware of my disgust for her, continued on.

"You know, you really should think about cutting your hair, and then maybe you could find a woman to settle down with," she said at the same time she went to reach up and grab my hair to show me why she thinks it was too long.

I grabbed her hand and gently put it back near her own body and said, "Thank you, Sicily. I'll definitely take that into consideration, but really, I must go."

"Yes, you probably do running that big corporation you barely have time to come to our friends' dinners anymore," she said.

"Yes, I'm so sorry about that. Maybe the next time I'll be available. Have a great evening, Sicily, and give my best to your mother," I said.

"Will do, Nate, although I'm not sure she'll remember you, ya know, with her declining age and all."

"I understand. See ya later."

I walked as fast as I could possibly walk to get away while I had the opening. I prayed to the gods above to please just let me finish this store run and get out of here before anyone else runs into me.

Chapter 22

Callie

Waking in the morning, I rolled over to see the time and realized it was 10:00 a.m. Wow, I never sleep in, and I feel completely rested. That's new. I stretched, climbed out of bed, and remembered I had a date with Nate Owens tonight. I don't regret accepting the date, which surprises me. I really am more nervous with anticipation of what's to come. Is he going to kiss me again tonight? God, I hope so. I could do that every day. It felt so good kissing him. I feel like listening to music while I drink my coffee this morning. I'm in such a good mood.

Waiting for Layla, I got a text, and it was from Nate.

"Hey, beautiful, dress casual, shorts and a tank top, and bring a bathing suit."

What the hell, where is he taking me? I laughed. A pool party? Now I'm starting to get nervous. What if he wants to take me to a party with his friends or his family? Oh my god, no. I'm not ready for that.

"Umm, okay? What are we doing, Nate? I'm not quite sure I'm ready for a crowded area with children and swimwear." Maybe I shouldn't have accepted this date.

I shot Layla a text before she headed my way with makeup and dresses.

"Layla, he told me to wear shorts, a tank top, and to bring a swimsuit. I'm not ready to meet his friends. I can't go to a crowded area with children. I can't."

My phone dinged, and I grabbed it, expecting it to be Layla, but it was Nate.

"Relax, beautiful, and take a breath. It'll just be you and I going to a special place. I promise you'll love it."

Okay, Callie, just breathe. You freaked out for no reason. Girl, just breathe. It's just a simple date, just you and Nate.

"Okay, Nate, I'm trusting you."

Let me shoot Layla a text explaining.

"Layla, he says we're going somewhere, just the two of us, and I'll love it. Are you almost here?"

"I'm on my way, girl. Five minutes, okay?" I got back from Layla.

"All right, Layla, doors unlocked."

I went to my closet and started tossing stuff out, trying to find something that would look good on me. In the middle of my meltdown, I heard, "Damn, girl, a tornado hit your room." I jumped, startled like hell.

"Jeez, Layla, give a girl some warning. I can't find anything cute to wear! What am I going to do?"

"Relax, Callie. First, let's leave this train wreck for a second, okay? I've got just what you need. Now follow me."

"A freaking shot, Layla, really?" I said louder than I intended too.

"Calm down, Callie. We're not getting blitzed. We're taking two shots. Just enough tequila to calm your nerves, girl. Now, lick, drink, lime."

"I haven't forgotten how to take a tequila shot, Layla. I'll play it your way for now, but if you pull out a joint, I'm out," and that line caused us both to laugh.

"Okay, that's better, girl. Now let's go back and find you something to wear. Do you still have that hot pink bikini?"

"Yeah, but don't you think that's a bit revealing for a first date?" I laughed.

"Uh, hell, no, I do not! Flaunt what you got! You are a beautiful woman."

"If you say so. I'm a little nervous about wearing that. I'm not near as skinny as I was when I bought that suit."

"You look better now with the little bit of weight, Callie. Trust me. That's the bathing suit you want. Now onto the outfit. Do you still have the dark wash jean shorts with the holes near the pockets?"

"I think so. Let me check my drawer. Yes, right here."

"All right, place them there, and let me see your shirts. Hmm… try this on."

Thank God for Layla. This is perfect. I look good. I forgot how good the shorts make my butt look. I put my swimsuit on under my clothes, came out, and did a twirl for Layla.

"Perfect, girl, you look hot!"

I was in dark wash jean shorts with a neon green off-the-shoulder shirt and my hot pink swimsuit underneath. We finished the outfit off with my black sandals that wrapped around the foot, and you could wear them in the water if necessary.

Layla headed out after a quick pep talk about protection and a tutorial on giving oral sex, which I know how to do. Damn her. I swear, I'm not as innocent as Layla makes me out to be. I decided to sit outside on the porch swing while I waited for Nate. I brought a lemonade out and scrolled through my social media, catching up on everything from today. I looked up when I heard a car coming and watched Nate pull in my drive. I stayed on the swing and watched him get out and walk toward me. I wondered how the hell I got so lucky to have ended up on this man's radar. I snapped out of my thoughts when I felt his hands pull me up and into a hug. I gave a small squeal and giggled while Nate seemed to be inhaling my hair. I laughed and asked what the hell he was doing.

"You smell so delicious. I can't help myself."

"You're ridiculous." I laughed and looked away, knowing my face was beet red.

"Come on. We better get going so we get there before the sun sets so you see your surprise. I hope you like nature."

We got buckled and headed out to whatever he had in store for us.

Chapter 23

Callie

The drive started off awkward, like there was this electric charge filling the cab of the car waiting to be released. Nate broke the silence by asking if I'd ever played twenty questions. I hadn't, but I knew what it was from hearing about it from my friends.

"I'll play your game, Mr. Smooth."

He laughed at that and said, "You go first, beautiful, before I pull this car over and kiss you senseless."

I blushed at that and looked down, thinking of something to ask.

"Do you have a favorite color?"

"I do," he responded, "its blue. How about you, beautiful?"

"I like the rainbow or all colors, if you will, except the color brown."

"Hmm…all colors, huh? Except brown. That's good to know. I do believe it's my turn now. What's your favorite food?" he asked.

"Oooh, that's a difficult one, but I'd have to go with Italian. What about yours?"

"Well, I like steak and seafood. They're my all-time favorite," Nate said and then winked at me before looking back to the road.

We went over twenty questions before Nate finally said, "We're here, beautiful. I hope you like what I've planned."

I am so nervous. I'm not sure what I'm supposed to do since this is so new to me.

"I'm sure I'll love it."

"Are you ready to start our beautiful night?"

"I believe I am."

"Okay, milady, shall we?"

I giggled, wrapping my arm through his as he led us down a windy trail through the woods. I giggled and asked if he was secretly taking me out here to kill me with no witnesses.

"I guess we'll find out because we're here."

I turned my head from him and looked in front of me, and what I saw was absolutely breathtaking! I was in shock. I felt his fingers reach under my chin and closed my mouth.

"You like it, I'm guessing. I did good?"

"Oh my god, Nate, how did you find this place?" I asked, really looking around me.

He shrugged his shoulders and said, "Its land my dad bought for my mother. She loved nature, and this was her favorite spot to bring us kids when we were small."

"Wow, I don't know what to say. Thank you for sharing this with me. It's beautiful."

"It's beautiful like you, and I wanted to show you that beauty is all around us. You just have to allow people to show you."

I looked around again, taking in the beauty and the detail Nate put into this space to show me he was serious about going over the top for me. He brought me to a freaking waterfall, complete with a natural hot water springs connected. He had tiny solar lights strung from the trees all around the fall, a blanket sprawled out under a beautiful weeping willow tree. He even had white, pink, and red rose petals thrown all over the ground, making it smell absolutely divine. I looked over at the blanket and two bottles of champagne chilling in a bucket with two glasses, along with a cheese and fruit platter. I also saw a meat and cheese platter as well.

"This is too much, Nate. You didn't have to do all this just for me."

"You're right. I didn't, but I wanted to. I want you to know that you are worth everything, and I'm willing to offer it if you'll accept it."

"It's not that I don't want to. I'm scared. I've only ever loved one man, and I made a promise to him that I am breaking as we speak. I am trying. I promise I am. I want to explore this chemistry between us and see where it leads us. I just need to take it day by day, if that's okay with you."

"We can take it however you need to. I'm not going anywhere."

"How do you always know the right thing to say, huh?" I said as I reached over, effectively grabbing onto his arm and pulling him to me. I leaned up on my toes and said, "Nate, will you kiss me?"

"You really need to ask," he said and sealed our lips in a toe-curling kiss. One that is just as good if not better than our first kiss. We pulled apart, both of us panting, staring at each other, and turned on at this point. Nate cleared his throat and asked, "Do you want to eat first or try out the hot springs?"

Well, that wasn't what was on my mind, I wanted to say, but I thought it was probably a good thing Nate slowed us down. I'm not sure what I want at this point, but I do know I want this man more than anything right now.

"How about a glass of that delicious-looking champagne over there and a soak in the springs for now?" I responded.

"Okay, perfect. You go ahead and get ready, and I'll pour us a glass of bubbly."

I felt a bit insecure with my suit, but Layla promised I looked sexy as hell in it, so I'm trusting her. I stripped out of my shorts and shirt, leaving me in this tiny pink bikini, waiting for Nate to turn around. I slowly made my way over to the springs and started to climb in when I felt a hand on my lower back and breath on my ear.

"Are you trying to seduce me, beautiful? Because it's working," he said.

I quickly giggled and said, "No way. My friend Layla made me wear it."

"Well, I should send your friend a thank-you note. This bikini was made for you. You look amazing in it."

I have no doubt my face is as red as rubies right now, so I quickly looked down and started climbing in, attempting not to fall in. Nate climbed in behind me, pulled me to him, and handed me a glass of champagne before he claimed my lips once more. Pulling away, I took a sip of my bubbly and laid my head on his shoulder since he was pretty much almost sitting. I decided to swim toward the waterfall, ducking under the water and swimming out a bit. I came up for air, completely mesmerized by the amazing feeling of a hot spring and a beautiful waterfall. I got under the waterfall and just let the water cascade over me. It felt so amazing. I felt so free and happy at this moment, something I hadn't felt in a long time. No numbness, no memories of my past traumas, no Jake, no nothing. It was just me and this happy memory I was creating with this waterfall right here, right now. Before I knew what was happening, Nate was by my side.

"What's wrong, beautiful?"

"What are you talking about?"

"You're crying, Callie."

"I didn't even realize it." I laughed. "They're happy tears, I think. I haven't felt this happy in so long, it overwhelmed me, I guess. Thank you for giving me this memory, Nate. You never know what you need until you get it, I guess."

Nate's arms wrapped around me, and his head nuzzled in the crook of my neck with my arms wrapped around his neck.

"Trust me, this is one of the most amazing memories I've ever been given the opportunity to have," Nate whispered while giving a quick kiss on my neck.

"You do know you're setting the bar high for yourself, right?" I laughed and splashed him, quickly diving under to get as far as I could before I felt a hand clamp on my foot, pulling me back against a chest. Squealing, I kicked my feet playfully while Nate dunked us both underwater. We splashed and played like two toddlers in a pool for quite a while before climbing out and under that willow tree to snack and refill our glasses.

Chapter 24

Callie

After ensuring we were full, Nate stood up, offered his hand, and asked me to follow him for my final surprise of the night. He led me through the trees and vines before I saw a stunning rustic cabin. You wouldn't even know it was hidden here.

"That's my mother's getaway house, but it's not exactly our destination," Nate said and gave my hand a gentle squeeze, leading me behind the beautiful little cabin. What I spotted behind it was even more breathtaking than the waterfall and hot springs. A makeshift bed fully equipped with a white comforter and a ton of pillows sprawled out in front of a huge projector screen. Around the area were tiny little white flowers and more solar lights giving the area romantic vibes. I threw my head back and laughed. Looking over, I saw Nate's expression was looking quite confused right now.

"Do you not like it? Oh shit, you don't watch TV, do you?" he said.

I stopped laughing and walked up to him, putting my hand on his chest.

"Yes, Nate, I absolutely do watch TV. I just laughed because nobody has ever done something so sweet and over the top for me. That's all."

"Well, I'm glad I could be of service. Now I hope you like the wedding crashers because that's all I could find on such short notice and no Wi-Fi out here."

"Wedding Crashers is fine, thank you," I said, giving him a sweet, gentle thank-you kiss. We cuddled under the blanket on the amazing pillows, finishing our date under the moon and stars, just him and I in this beautiful, secluded place. I wondered why I couldn't just let this man in. He really is amazing. I felt a kiss on the crown of my head before blackness overtook me, and I fell into the most amazing restful sleep I've had in a long time.

Nate

The credits rolled along the screen, and I had yet to wake this glorious, beautiful creature in my arms. I stayed in this position for a long time, considering Callie fell asleep within the first twenty-five minutes of the movie. My arm was numb at this point, and my back was killing me, but for some reason, I couldn't make myself move for fear it'd wake her and end our evening together. I knew, at some point, I'd have to wake her up and take her home, but for now, I'm enjoying watching her while she sleeps. Maybe it's a little creepy, but I can't help myself. Her beauty really is amazing. It's like being awestruck by a famous star you've always wanted to meet, and you freeze completely. No words come to mind. Your body parts are completely nonfunctional, and you're like stuck in this weird form, looking like some crazy lunatic that someone should call security for.

Weird analogy, I know, but that's the best I can give you of how I feel being around her sometimes. When I pulled into her drive this evening, it was like a scene from a movie, watching her swing back and forth on her porch swing while drinking her lemonade, waiting for me to show up to get her. Seeing her in those tight short shorts that made her ass look freaking absolutely amazing and that neon green shirt, I couldn't even tell you the thoughts running through my head at that moment. When she noticed I was basically inhaling her hair into my nostrils, I thought she might tell me to get lost, but she didn't, and, man, was I thankful for that. I didn't mean to be weird. I just couldn't help myself. She is intoxicating. I wanted nothing more than to cancel this date and take her inside on the first available wall, bed, floor, whatever was closest.

When we got to the waterfall and I got to see her reaction to my mom's hiding spot, I knew I'd made the best decision by creating our first date here. I couldn't take my eyes off her. When she shed the little clothing she had on, it was almost a breaking point for me. It took everything, all my strength, not to initiate something I knew damn well she wasn't ready for, so I settled for kissing her instead. When I joined her under the waterfall and saw her tears, I wondered what I had done now to make her cry. It seemed like that's all I made her do around me. But when she said they were happy tears, I was mentally high-fiving myself for giving her this happy moment.

When she cuddled against me after reassuring me she did like TV, I couldn't help but wrap my arms around her and promise myself I'd protect her from any more pain. I'd do what's necessary to shield her from any unwarranted negatives the world throws. I needed to wake her up though. I really have to stretch my arm and back before I lose all circulation.

"Hey, beautiful, Callie, hey, you have to wake up. Movie's over."

"Five more minutes. I'm still tired, and I was having a wonderful dream," she said while peeking one eye open at me. I laughed and started sitting us up gently since I couldn't feel my arm at this point.

"I'm sorry I fell asleep, Nate. I guess I was more exhausted than I realized."

"Not a problem at all. I actually enjoyed having you cuddled next to me, mumbling my name in your sleep. It really does wonders for a man's ego, you know."

Callie

"Shut up." I laughed. "You're so stupid. I never called out for you. I was dreaming about the actors in the movie. Thank you."

"If you say so, beautiful, but I heard, 'Oh, yes, Nate, right there. Please don't stop.'"

My face was four shades of red at this point, and I wished I could crawl under a rock, never to be seen. How embarrassing that I talk in my sleep, especially while calling out for the man I'm with at the moment.

"I did not. You're lying."

"Am I?" he said as he threw that stupid smirk and raised his eyebrow at me. I just hugged his neck and hid my head on his shoulder. "Nothing to be embarrassed about. You know, I dream of you, and I can tell you that the things I'm dreaming are definitely not PG-rated."

All I could do was stuff my head farther in the crook of his neck. I knew I was as red as a ruby jewel. Nate let out a boisterous laugh, and I couldn't help but laugh with him.

"You make it so easy to tease you, girl, my gosh."

"I know, and I can't help it, so knock it off, will ya?"

"Fine, fine, we'd better get this show on the road. It's getting late."

"What time is it anyway?"

"Ten thirty p.m., sweets."

"Oh my, that's way later than I usually stay up," and again, Nate's laughter was contagious.

"Will you stop laughing at me? I'm a busy woman, you know, and people expect me to be on their scheduled time."

"I know, and I'm sorry for laughing. It's just you said that like some eighty-five-year-old little old lady."

"I most certainly did not, and quite frankly, I'm offended," I responded and did my best to keep a very unsure, offended look on my face.

"I didn't mean it. Come on. Don't be mad, beautiful. It was just a joke."

I burst into laughter, unable to hide my feelings any longer.

"You little snake, you," he said and attacked me with a tickling fest.

"O-ooh m-my gosh, N-N-Nate, p-p-p-pleaseeee stopp!"

"Say I'm the handsomest in the world."

"I promise you're the handsomest man I know right now."

"Okay. I'll take that," he said and offered me a hand. "Truce?"

"Yes, sir, truce," and I shook his hand only to be pulled into a quick sweet, gentle kiss and a hug after.

"All right, we really should be getting you home, grandma."

"Hey! We truced!"

"I'm sorry, okay, okay, that's it. I had one last one, I swear."

"You better be!"

When we pulled into the driveway, I was not sure either of us was ready to end the night. It had been magical in a sort of way. I had never had anyone invest that much effort into impressing me. Usually, it was me trying to impress someone enough to get the job.

"I definitely enjoyed myself. You gave me plenty of happy memories, and that's the best thing to happen to me in a long time."

"I want to make you happy every day, Callie. Let me take you on a second date, please?"

"I think you've done plenty this evening to deserve a second date, Nate, so yes."

"Great. I've got it all planned already, well, kind of."

"You're such a dork, Owens! What were you going to do if I said no, huh?"

"I don't know." He laughed. "I hadn't thought that far ahead."

"No? Just far enough to plan a second date already," I said with my eyebrow raised. We both started laughing at that.

"Touché, my lady, touché."

"All righty, I've got to work early, so I'm going to go now. Thank you so much for the great night." I reached my hand over and caressed his cheek and pulled him into a passion-filled sweet kiss, pouring all the emotions I have from this date into it.

"If I get treated like that at the end of our dates, I'll take you on one every night if you're available." He laughed.

I threw a wink and watched him pull away. After I closed the door, effectively locking it behind me, I kicked off my shoes and headed for my bed, opting to just go straight to sleep and wash the sheets and shower tomorrow morning.

Chapter 25

Callie

The next month went by extremely slow. Nate and I were both slammed with business meetings and, of course, the renovation for Bustling Corp on my end. We barely had time to even text each other, let alone have a conversation that existed of anything besides the renovation. My evenings were spent relaxing and talking with Layla at least twice a week. I really did mean it when I said I was going to be a better friend for her. But it's finally the day Nate and I are going to have that second date. He was due to pick me up at five, and it was currently 3:30 p.m., and Layla had yet to show me this new design she was putting on me tonight. So far, I had fuchsia-colored eyeshadow and bright lipstick.

"Layla, I feel a bit like a hooker. Are these really the colors we're using? Please tell me it's a joke, right?"

"Girl, you look fantastic and nothing like a hooker. It will match the dress perfectly. Trust me!"

"I do trust you obviously, but I'm struggling with so much color on my face."

"Oh, hush, you'll like it when it's completed."

"Okay, okay, Layla. Just hurry. I'm getting antsy."

"Callie, I'm done with your makeup. Will you just hold your horses?" Layla laughed.

Layla had me close my eyes and promise I'd keep them closed until I was in the dress and it fit perfectly before looking.

"Okay, just one more second, Callie. Put your arm through here. Uh-huh, that's it. Now let me zip it."

"Oh, Callie, I knew this would look amazing on you!" Layla gushed.

I opened my eyes and gasped out loud at what I saw! The dress was a perfect fit. It was short with a piece of waist that attached to make a long train in the back. It was completely open in the back, and the front was cut so low all the way between my breasts down to my waist. It was black with fuchsia-colored flowers designed perfectly all the way around the entire gown.

"Layla, I say, this dress is amazing! Are you sure you want me to be the first to wear this design?"

"Of course, girl! I wouldn't have put it on anyone but you. It fits you like a glove. Now get your perfume on and finish your breathing since we both know you will, and I'm gonna go before your date gets here. I expect details down to the T, Callie Marie! I love you. Have fun," she sang as she was walking out the door.

I stood there, looking at myself, thinking, how in the hell does she make me look so beautiful? I don't even recognize myself.

I was so engrossed in what I saw in the mirror that I forgot to add my perfume, and Nate was here since I heard the doorbell.

"Shit," I said and scrambled around, adding perfume and a bit more deodorant, and raced to the door.

I was extremely disappointed to see George there at my door and not Nate.

"Hello, miss," George said. "Are you ready to go?"

"I am, George, and I'm sorry if this comes out rude, but where is Nate?"

George gave a small humorous laugh and said, "No offense taken, ma'am, and I can't reveal that. I was instructed to pick you up and bring you to your destination this evening."

"Okay, then I say, I guess let's get this show on the road. Not exactly what I had in mind, Nate," I mumbled to myself.

George heard me, of course, and reassured me. "Ma'am, if I may."

"Callie, George, just Callie, please, I say."

"Yes, of course, Callie. You will not be disappointed by any means. Boss went above and beyond tonight. I've never seen him do this for any woman, and trust me, there's a lot that would want to lock him down. He only has eyes for you."

"George, you're a good employee, and I sure hope Nate considers you a friend as well. Thank you for making me feel better."

We both stayed quiet for the remainder of the drive, with me trying to decipher anything George said that could be a hint as to what Nate had planned.

We pulled up to this tall building that I'd never seen before, and George walked me in the doors and said, "Go all the way to the top, Callie. Your journey begins there for the evening."

"Okay, thank you so much, George. I hope you have a great night as well."

All the way to the top, I felt so nervous. Forty-five *ding*, forty-six *ding*, forty-seven *ding*, my hands were getting so sweaty, and there was nowhere for me to wipe them. If I wiped them on my dress, it might leave a streak of wetness. Finally, the elevator stopped on floor 52.

Walking out, I was hit with the most amazing view. There was a tent set up with twinkling fairy lights, pink and white tulle draped with real pink with white mixed flowers sewn into it. Underneath all the beauty was a dance floor equipped with a man playing romantic soft music on the piano. In the far corner was a table set up for two, and I couldn't be more shocked and amazed by how much effort Nate had put into this date. If I thought the first date was amazing and this second date was already wowing me, I don't know what a third would look like.

All of a sudden, I felt a shiver up my spine and a crackle of energy all around me. I felt breath on my neck and heard the words, "You take my breath away, Mrs. Callie Marie Palet. I'm speechless. Really, your beauty never ceases to amaze me."

I turned around and whispered, "Nate, this is absolutely breathtaking. I love it!"

"This is only the beginning," Nate said and gave me a gentle kiss on the lips while guiding me to the dance floor. "Just the Way You Look Tonight" by Frank Sinatra started playing by the piano man.

Nate grabbed my hands and moved them up his chest and around his neck. All the while, he was sliding one hand down my face and arm, and the other was sliding down to the small of my back.

I shivered and just stared at Nate's handsome face.

"I could do this forever," Nate said. "But I'm afraid we'll miss out on the food if we don't sit and order. I've called in a renowned chef, and he's prepared to offer us a couple of different options," Nate told me as he guided us to the table, pulling my chair out for me before getting himself seated.

No longer did we sit, a waiter showed up. I didn't even see him, nor did I know he was there. I was so focused on Nate.

We were offered beef Wellington, chicken Madeira, Alfredo, or a surf and turf.

I ordered the beef Wellington, and Nate, of course, ordered the surf and turf.

Nate looked amazing in a black suit with a dark green tie that accentuated his eyes. He looked absolutely divine tonight. As we finished our dinner, Nate walked me to the gated edge and said, "I've got a surprise for you, beautiful."

"A surprise, huh? It really isn't necessary, Nate. I don't even deserve half of the nice things you do for me."

"Shhh, no negative words," he whispered in my ear. "Just watch the view."

As soon as he finished saying that, the sky lit up with an amazing fireworks show.

"Nate, thank you for this," I said as the tears fell down my cheeks.

"Why are you crying, sweets? Are these happy tears or sad?"

"Both, I think, Nate. I haven't seen fireworks shows in over six years now. I lost the kids six and a half years ago, and this is the first time I'm seeing fireworks again. I've heard them, of course, but never have I gone to a show after my kids passed."

"It's going to be okay, Callie. I'm so thankful I was the one to share this moment with you."

The ride home was quiet but not awkward. I think we were both just reflecting on the beautiful date and the way it played out.

"Thank you for another amazing date and night, Nate. I really enjoyed myself this evening."

"There's more nights in your future that look like this, Callie, if you want them to. The ball is in your court now. Choose me, and you'll always be cherished and never have any doubts that you're enough for me."

"Thank you, Nate, and I promise I'm trying, okay?"

With a sweet, gentle kiss that turned fiery in a second, I pulled away with one last kiss to Nate's cheek and told him, "Have a great rest of your evening, Nate."

Chapter 26

Callie

Layla had been begging me to come to this birthday party for her friend from college's brother at a local bar we used to hang out at. I was torn, only because I owed Layla; however, it was the only night Nate was free for the evening, and it just so happened to be his birthday. After discussing this with Nate and realizing that his family had a party planned for him that he was going to ditch, I shut that nonsense down.

"Absolutely not, Nate! You have no idea what it means to have a family who supports you and wants to throw you an amazing birthday party. You are not canceling or ditching this party for me. We can wait until we're both free again. It's not that serious, besides Layla has been begging me to come with her to this party she has been invited to. I'll probably have a drink or two and come back home to soak in my tub and relax."

"Ugh! Again, I'm jealous of the water and your bathtub. It seems that bathtub gets more time with you than I do."

I laughed and shoved him out my door. "Go home, Nate. Get ready for your party, and I'll see you tomorrow."

"All right, beautiful, but I won't pretend I'm happy about this. Are you sure you won't just come then since you're making me go?"

"No, I will not intrude on a party I'm sure your family has been planning for a long time for you. Another time, Nate. Now go home so I can get myself ready as well. Layla will kill me if I make her late, even though she's fashionably late to most everything," I laughed.

"Okay, but before I go, how about a birthday kiss for the birthday boy, huh?"

"You're so childish." I laughed but grabbed him and pulled him in for a kiss, which I tried to make short and sweet, but somebody had other plans and brought me into a fifteen-minute make-out session.

I quickly showered and shot Layla a message, letting her know I'd be ready in forty-five minutes. Before I even had time to put makeup on, my doorbell was ringing.

"Delivery for a Callie Palet."

"This is her."

"Here ya go. Have a great night," he said and walked away, leaving me staring at the most beautiful bouquet of lilies. I almost got the door closed before my sweet Layla barged through it.

"Hey, girl, who sent the flowers? Mr. Romantic?" she asked while wiggling her eyebrows.

"Actually, I don't know." I laughed. "I literally just got them placed in my hand before you barged in, taking over the place," I said and rolled my eyes at her for dramatics.

"Oh, hush, you know you are happy to see me. I couldn't leave you here by yourself to get dressed without my opinion. You know darn well you'd be texting saying, 'Layla, what should I wear?'"

"Maybe, maybe not, Layla, you never know," and we both laughed. I grabbed the card and gently opened the tiny little envelope, pulled it out, and began to read it.

Dearest Callie,

You owe me a third date. If I remember correctly, you said you'd think about a third date. But you have yet to provide said date, therefore I am cashing in on that date tomorrow evening at 4 p.m. I've cleared my schedule just for you. Please dress in a gown of your choice. I've got the evening all planned out.

Nate

"Layla, he's taking me on a third date tomorrow evening and asked that I wear a gown. You still down to let me borrow one of your designs?"

"Hell, yes, girl, do you even need to ask? What time? And I'll be here with my hair and makeup artists and the gown."

"He's picking me up at 4:00 p.m. Will that work?"

"Absolutely!" she sang. "Now let's get you ready for tonight, shall we?"

After an hour and I was serious, we finally decided on a black leather miniskirt for Layla with a red off-the-shoulder silk shirt, and let me tell you, she looked hot as hell. For me, we decided on a silky black jumper pantsuit, and we paired it with my thick red belt at the waist and a really cute short black leather jacket. We both had amazing smoky eyes that accentuated our outfits and red lipstick. I'd say we were going to turn heads tonight. I quickly sent Nate a selfie of myself in the mirror.

"Hey, handsome, all ready for my night with Layla! How do I look?"

To which he immediately responded, "Are you kidding me, beautiful? You really needed to ask if you looked good. That's a definite hell, yes, baby! So good, in fact, I really think I should come find you tonight, or I may lose my mind wondering if every man's eyes are on you this evening."

I laughed, and Layla snatched my phone from me and shot him a quick text herself.

"Hey, Mr. Romantic, Layla here, and I'm here to say if you dare track her down, I'll have your head on a stick. She deserves this night. Don't ruin it!"

"Oh my god, Layla, why would you message that? He was just being flirty. I'm sure he wouldn't have tracked me down tonight."

"Girl, you really don't think that he is going to see you this hot and not worry about other men trying to take what he's working on with you?"

"And what would he be working on, huh?" I said angrily.

"Stop it, Callie, and quit being mad at me. That is not the way I meant it, and you know it. I'm merely saying that he has eyes and knows that men will see you tonight and want to dance or get your attention tonight. He wants you, and I mean, he wants you in every sense of the word. He wouldn't waste his time creating that dreamy, steamy date at the waterfall and hot springs or the rooftop and fireworks if he didn't. The fact that he hasn't tried to get in your pants besides a few hints, never any pushy prompts. I'm just saying I'd be worried, too, especially if he's yet to ask you to be his girlfriend."

I stood there stupefied, staring at my only friend, wondering how the hell I never thought about any of this before now. Not having time to process it, my phone pinged. Knowing it was Nate, I opened it up.

"Hello, best friend of Callie's. It's nice to meet you. While I can assure you that I will not be happy at the thought of other men having their eyes on my beautiful flower, I will most definitely not ruin her evening. Have more faith in me and know I also understand she needs to gain her confidence and become herself through her own choices. Never in a million years would I cause turmoil in her life. Now I hope you enjoy your night, beautiful, and I hope you text me when you get home. I'll be thinking of you all night, and I have saved this selfie so I may come back and see your face when I'm bored this evening."

"Well, I'll be damned, Callie Marie, you really have found your Prince Charming, haven't you?"

"I told you, Layla, you shouldn't have thought him a villain tonight. He really does seem great, doesn't he?" I sighed.

"Mmhmm, now let's go, chicka. We've got a party to attend, and we're already going to be fashionably late."

Lucky for us, Layla had her driver bring us because there was no parking at the local bar. People were lined up down the street as far as you could see, which is pretty common for a Saturday night, being it's the only bar in our town. Layla had such confidence she could take over a room with just a smile and a polite hello, and then it was all eyes on her. So I was definitely a little nervous coming here with so many people. This used to be something both of us would do together once a month before the accident, but it had been almost seven years since I'd gone out to anything like this.

My hands were sweaty, and my heart was beating so fast I felt like it was going to burst out of my chest any second.

"Okay, Callie Marie, bottoms up, girl."

"What the hell is it, Layla?"

"Doesn't matter, girl. You need to calm down a bit, and this will help you do just that."

"Oh my god, that burns so bad. I feel like I just burned a hole all the way down my esophagus into my stomach. What the hell was that seriously?"

"Just a little whiskey. We're going to sit here for a minute until the shot kicks in."

"Yeah, okay, Layla, but I'm never taking one of those ever again. It still burns."

"Oh, you big baby. Drink some water, but not a lot. Just a sip or it'll sober you up."

"So bossy, jeez. You're lucky I love you, Layla Jane Snider!"

"Awe, that's so sweet."

"I know, right," she responded with a lot of fluttering of her eyes.

"Jerk face." I laughed. "Now we can go. I'm ready."

"Are you sure, Callie? We can wait a bit longer if you want."

"Nope. I'm ready. Let's go. Rip off the Band-Aid, right, Layla?"

"Now you're talking, girl! Let's get this party started, shall we? There ain't no party if I'm not there." She laughed. She really isn't lying. Layla can bring any party up with her personality and any kind of booze. She seems like she drinks a lot, but she really doesn't. She can have a few drinks and quit but still have a fabulous night. One of her many talents. Me, on the other hand, I never really drank, so a couple of drinks, and I'm toasty and relaxed.

Walking into the bar, the first thing I noticed was it was loud as hell and over in the corner. There were about fifteen guys all hollering, "Shots, shots, shots!"

There was a girl on the end of the bar doing body shots off her friend. At least, I think it's her friend. There were a couple of people grinding on each other out on the dance floor and a couple of others making out pretty heavily, groping each other right out where anyone could see. Layla and I looked at each other and busted out laughing.

"Nothing ever changes with the bar life, does it?" I said.

"No, I guess not. Come on. Let's go find an empty spot at the bar and get some drinks."

"All right, let's do it."

After five minutes, we finally got up to the bar to get a drink, and I heard, "Well, holy shit, if it ain't Callie freaking Marie! I haven't seen you in ages. Sherry, Sherry!"

"What, Michael? I'm talking to Caitlyn!"

"Look who I just found."

"Oh my god, Callie? Who got you out of your house? I mean, how did you get here? I mean, my god, it's been so long. You wouldn't respond to my calls or my texts or answer your door. I thought you'd come around when you were ready, but it's been two years. You look so good, Callie Marie!"

"Thank you, Sherry! Good to see you also, Michael. Yeah, about that, I'm really sorry. I was such a shitty friend. I'm working on that."

"Callie babe, what do you want to drink? Oh my god, Layla? You're the one who got her out of the house?"

"Well, had any of you bitches thought to hang around and just keep trying, you'd be right here celebrating with me and Callie Marie now, wouldn't you?"

"Hey, Layla, stop it. You know it's my fault I wouldn't even talk to anyone. What were they supposed to do, huh?"

"Not an excuse, Callie, for being shitty friends. You needed us, and they bailed when times got tough, and don't you dare ever tell me it's your fault your friends bailed again. Do you hear me, Callie Marie? Ever! That was their choice. True friends will remain by your side no matter what the circumstances are. Do you hear me?"

"Okay, Layla, okay. Damn, girl, chill. It wasn't like that, Layla, and you know it," Sherry said.

"Oh, yeah, Sherry, then please, please enlighten me on how it was. Please, by all means, the floor is yours," Layla said with a gesture of her hand.

"You can't be serious right now, Layla. What did you want us to do? Beg Callie to talk to us? Stay outside her door until she lets us in, damn!"

"That's exactly what you should have done, Sherry. I did! You bitches were supposed to be some of her truest, most trusted friends, and instead, every one of you morons left her when she needed us the most, and that is why I have nothing to say to any of you. Now if you'll excuse us, we're here to have a good time." Layla grabbed me and said, "Here. I ordered you a hurricane."

"That wasn't necessary, Layla. I know you blame them, but it's not all their fault."

"Uh-huh, I am not hearing this shit. We came here for a good time, and that's what we're going to do. Now come on. Let's go find my friend." With a tight grip on my wrist so we didn't get separated, we made our way toward the back of the bar to a private room that really wasn't very private, considering there was just as much chaos in this room as there was in the front of the bar.

"Lincoln, get your ass down!" I heard a girl scream, "Stop it! You're such a jerk."

"There's my girl," Layla yelled over the music. "Come on, Callie, I'll introduce you."

"Callie, this is one of my good friends, Katie. Katie, this is Callie."

"It's so nice to finally put a name to the face!" Katie said and gave me a small hug.

"This idiot here is Lincoln, my brother's best friend, but ignore him. He's a major womanizer!"

"I am not, and that's offensive, Kate!"

"Yeah, whatever, stupid, go away."

"You never say anything nice to me, and it hurts my feelings, Kate," Lincoln said with his hand sprawled over his heart.

"Lincoln, go the hell away. Go find my brother, would ya? And leave me the hell alone."

"Fine, you win, but just so you know, you've really broken my heart this time," he said while wiping a pretend tear from under his eye.

"I'm going to kill you, Lincoln!" Katie screamed, and he took off running, laughing like a typical boy.

"Gosh, you'd think a man would act his age, but apparently not," Katie said while giggling a bit. "So what are you ladies drinking? My parents are forking the bill for this here shit storm."

"I'm good for now, but thank you," I replied while lifting my drink to show her it was full.

"Cool, just let me know when you need one, and I'll flag down our waiter for tonight."

I shook my head and looked around. There were so many people in this room you could barely move. However, I spotted the one person who had been on my mind for the last month, Nate Owens. He was in the back, leaning on the wall with one foot kicked over the other, a beer in one hand, and his phone in the other. *Looks like he's texting*, I thought right at the same moment my phone vibrated alerting me of an incoming message.

"Hey, beautiful, I hope you and your friend are having a good time. I know I said I wouldn't bother you, but I couldn't help myself. I keep looking at this picture of you and wishing I was with you. I know I'm supposed to have fun celebrating my birthday with my family, but I see them all the time, and honestly, I miss you, sweets. Maybe I've had a few too many drinks, but I figure nothing wrong in telling you that I want you and plan on making you mine in the near future, so be ready, my flower. Text me when you're home safe. Nate."

Holy shit balls! This man's able to bring me to my knees with just a freaking text.

"Hey, yourself, handsome. We are having a great time. In fact, so great that I'm looking at one of the hottest guys I've ever laid eyes on, hoping that he'll see me too."

I couldn't even help myself from teasing him, considering he hadn't even taken his eyes off his phone since I spotted him. He literally had no idea I was looking at him. I saw him take a big pull from his beer and switch legs, looking like he might be a bit angry right now that I couldn't even help myself but giggle.

"Hmm, I think you're pulling my leg, beautiful, since you told me I was the handsomest, you know."

I laughed and grabbed Layla by the arm.

"Layla, I think Katie is Nate's sister."

"No way, girl. Her last name isn't Owens. It's Clouse."

"I'm telling you, Layla. Look at the man against the back wall leaning on it, glaring at his phone." I laughed. "That's my Nate, and I've just made him jealous by telling him I was staring at one of the hottest guys I've ever seen." I laughed.

"Damn, girl, you harsh." Layla laughed. "Katie, Katie!"

"Yeah, what's up, Layla?"

"What's your brother's name?"

"Nate, why?"

"Well, I'll be damned, girl. Your brother has the major hots for my girl Callie, even took her on a date to your mother's waterfall."

"No shit, really? He's never brought anyone there. That's kind of a sacred place for him since our mom died."

"But I thought you said your parents were forking the bill here tonight?"

"I did, my dad and his wife. Our mom died ten years ago of a heart attack, and my dad remarried."

"Oh shit, I'm so sorry, Katie, I didn't know."

Katie shrugged her shoulders and said, "You wouldn't. It's not something we go around announcing."

"I get it, and I'm sorry I brought it up."

"No worries. Now does my brother know you're here yet?"

"No, but we're texting, and I better text him back before he loses his shit from my last message." I laughed.

"Perfect. Come on, ladies. I've got some fun I need to have."

"Wait, I'm not sure I want to make him angry."

"Oh, girl, come on! A little fun never hurt anyone. This is payback for the time he took my ex-husband out to a strip club for his bachelor party after I asked him not to."

"Okay, but we're not taking this to the edge. Do you two hear me?" I said.

"Fine, fine. We won't, I promise. I just want to mess with him a bit before he realizes you're here. I promise not to take it too far."

Chapter 27

Nate

God, this party blows. I sighed, taking another pull from my beer. Lincoln is, well, being Lincoln. Flirting with every girl he sees, including my sister. One of these days, she's going to clock his ass, and I'm going to sit back and laugh. I've warned him time and time again that Katie has a mean right hook, but it seems to go in one ear and out the other.

Everyone was talking, dancing, and having a good time, but I couldn't help but wonder what Callie was doing if she was having fun or thinking about me like I was her. Maybe I'll just shoot her a text, no harm in that.

After I texted her, basically putting it out there saying I wanted her, she responded back, saying she was looking at one of the hottest guys she'd ever met. What the fuck! I never wanted her to see any other man but me, so I won't lie and say my jealousy didn't show on my face. I responded back, telling her she was a fibber, and she left me on damn read.

I was getting anxious, waiting for her response. She looked hot as hell tonight, and I knew for a fact every guy would be looking her way.

My dad came over, asked me what was up, and handed me another beer. I just smiled and said, "Not much, pops, just taking a breather." He got called away, and yet I still haven't gotten a response from Callie. I really wanted to go find her and beat whoever it was she was looking at.

I finally decided I couldn't take it anymore and that I was going to go find her. Her friend be damned, and my phone dinged.

"I didn't fib. You are one of the handsomest, but this guy is like really, really hot! With his tight shirt on and his hair all nicely done. Yummo, it's very tempting since there's no other man here to curb my appetite."

What the hell is she talking about? That doesn't sound at all like the Callie I know. Is she completely drunk?

"Callie, are you okay? Did you have too much to drink? I'll come get you right now if you want me to."

There's no way I'm leaving her anywhere talking like that. Anyone could take advantage of her. And where the hell is her friend? She about took my damn head off for teasing. I'd come find her, yet I was getting raunchy text messages. Something's not right.

"Of course, I'm fine, silly. I've only had a couple of drinks before I found Mr. Sexy."

Mr. Sexy? What the hell is going on right now?

"That's it! Callie, where are you? I'm coming to get you right now."

Before I could take a step, my damn sister was behind me, grabbing my arm and getting everyone's attention.

"Everyone, I'd like to make a toast to my baby brother. Please gather around."

"Kate, can we please do this later? I have to go somewhere really quick."

"Umm, hell no, brother. It's only once you turn twenty-eight, you know."

"Yes, I know, Katie, but it's important, please?"

"Oh, stop it, Nate. Nothing is more important than your family. Now come on, get over here."

After twenty minutes of Katie rambling on and me getting not a single response from Callie, I was almost desperate to leave and go find her when I spotted her standing across the room, staring at me with a nervous look on her face and a petite blond, I'm assuming to be her friend, Layla, next to her smiling from ear to ear. Katie finished her speech, gave me a hug, and whispered in my ear, "About damn time you notice that beautiful woman is here," and laughed like a maniac.

"You're such an asshole, Kate!"

"Yeah, yeah, baby brother. You love me, and you know it! Now go get your girl, whom I very much approve of, by the way. She's an absolute doll and wouldn't let me dare message you one more time."

"I knew that wasn't her." I laughed. "It's nothing like the way she talks," I said.

"Exactly. That was the point, you idiot. And yet, you still took the bait."

"See ya later, sis. Got to go." I walked toward my girl, never losing eye contact. It took me a few minutes to get through the sea of people my parents invited, even though a lot of them I haven't talked to in ages, but who's going to say no to free booze? None of these morons who showed up, that's for sure. I finally made it to her and grabbed her, swung her around, and grabbed her lips in a passionate kiss. I'm not one for PDA, but with this girl, I needed anyone in the vicinity, man or woman, to know she was mine.

"I'm sorry," Callie said. "It really started as a joke. I thought you'd look around and see me, but then Katie and Layla realized who you were, and they took over. But I did stop them from any other messages. They made me promise to stand here until you noticed me."

"Callie, you have nothing to apologize for. Are you crazy? I am just so excited you're here with me because this party just got a hundred times better now that you're here. Let me get you a drink. What are you drinking?"

"Layla has been ordering me hurricanes."

"Hmm, a hurricane. Okay, I'll order that for you."

Callie

"You must be, Nate," Layla said, not even giving me a chance to properly introduce them and stuck her hand out, practically demanding him to acknowledge her.

"Ahh, and you must be Layla," Nate said while shaking her hand.

"You guessed right, and judging from the way you just greeted my girl, you want more than a friendship with her, am I correct?"

Nate looked at me, and I mouthed, "I'm sorry, but Layla seems to have lost her filter."

"You do know that my friend here is pretty innocent and that she's been through a lot. You'll have to teach her plenty of things, eventually."

"Layla, goddamn you, stop it!" I screamed and shoved her shoulder a bit.

"What, girl, I'm just speaking the truth! You know I've got your back always. If I thought for a second he was jacking you around, I'd cut off his balls," she said like it was nothing. I was so embarrassed.

"I'm so sorry, Nate," I said to him, who was laughing at this point. "Please excuse my friend. I think she's had a little too much to drink," I said with gritted teeth.

"Speak for yourself, girl. You know I'm not embarrassed to be myself, and you need someone to look after you so that nobody takes advantage of you."

"I'm an adult, Layla, and you know damn well nobody takes advantage of me because nobody gets close enough except Nate here, who seems to have busted through my walls." I looked at Nate, who held his hand out and asked for a dance.

"Of course," I said. "Although I'm not sure I remember how. It's been so long," I teased, "knowing we just danced on our date."

"Really, milady, then I guess you'll just have to follow my lead, and you'll be fine."

Right as we went out, a slow song came on, and Nate smiled like a Cheshire cat. "Just what I was hoping for," he said and pulled me close. As we swayed, he was whispering in my ear how beautiful I was and how I was the hottest girl he'd ever had the pleasure of dancing with. He asked if I'd let him and George drive me home.

"Of course, you can," I said, a bit slurred since I've already had more hurricanes than I could count and a shot. I was definitely feeling the alcohol.

Chapter 28

Nate

After we let her friend Layla know I was driving her home, she threatened my manhood again. I called George to have him meet us out front with the divider up since I couldn't seem to keep my hands off this beautiful, enticing woman. We got in, and it was like a massive magnetic pull we were together and trying to get as close as humanly possible.

Callie was on my lap, kissing me, running her hands up my neck and into my hair, and I was kissing her everywhere: her neck, her lips, her ears. When she moaned and ground down on my erection, I almost came undone. She felt so good, even with the clothes between us.

"God, I want you so bad, Callie. Just say the words, and I'll give you all the pleasure you need for tonight, I promise."

"Okay, Nate," she said in between kisses on my neck. I felt the car stop, and George knocked on the window, knowing not to interrupt by opening the door. I got out, holding Callie, and she wrapped her legs around my waist. While I walked up her porch steps, she was digging in her tiny little purse attached to her wrist for her key.

"I found it." She laughed, and I grabbed it, unlocked the door, and shut it with my foot, planting her right there on the wall and grinding up into her while pulling her jumper down and taking a nipple in my mouth. Callie moaned and threw her head back against the wall.

"More, Nate, please. I need you." She was grabbing my shirt, bunching it up, trying to get it off my head while I was desperately trying to get her damn clothes off her.

"Where the hell is the zipper on this damn thing?"

"Put me down. Let me help you get it off."

I must have blacked out because, for the life of me, I couldn't remember how the hell I got from that wall to her bed. It was morning, and this beautiful woman was naked next to me, wrapped in her sheets. How in the hell is it that the moment I've been waiting for with Callie has happened, and I cannot remember a single bit of it, minus the entrance into her house? I knew I was drunk, but damn, I never thought I was blackout drunk. I rolled over and gently moved a piece of hair off Callie's face so I could see the beautiful curve in her jaw to the most perfect slant of her nose, all the way to the gorgeous shape of her eyes. God, I really am a lucky son of a bitch to be lying next to this amazing woman who has conquered all that this life has thrown at her. I backed off a bit as she started moving a little.

Callie

Waking up, I started to move and groaned from the uncomfortable pain I felt in my thighs and lady parts. "What the hell happened last night?" I groaned. "I'm going to kill Layla!"

"Good morning, beautiful." I heard and jumped up quickly to a sitting-up position, completely, not realizing I was fully naked under my blankets.

"How did you get in here, Nate?"

"Umm…you don't remember last night either, I'm taking it?"

"Oh my god," I said and slapped my hand over my mouth. "Holy shit, Nate, I remember you bringing me home and making out in the car, but everything else is a complete blur."

"Uh, not that I don't appreciate the view, sweets, but you might want to cover it up, considering my friend is at attention from the view."

I looked down, and to my complete ignorant embarrassment, I threw myself backward, pulling the blankets over my head while I was at it.

"Can you give me a minute to get decent, please?"

"Absolutely, beautiful, but first," he said, pulling the blanket off my face, "don't be embarrassed. I completely enjoyed the view, just knew you'd react this way," and he sweetly kissed my lips and stood up.

He stood as naked as the day he was born, his cock completely full mast and saluting me to the point it could have high-fived my forehead.

Nate winked and said, "Close your mouth, sweetheart, before something wanders in," and grabbed his clothes, quietly shutting my door on his way out.

Oh my god, I had sex. Oh my god, what do I do? I found myself repeating over and over again to myself. What if we didn't use protection? I raced to the bathroom on that thought, and sure enough, there was a condom disposed of in my trash bin. Okay, Callie, breathe. You used protection. It's okay. There is nothing wrong with you having sex.

God, why am I like this? Jake is dead, my kids are dead, and they're not coming back. I'm allowed to have a life. "Get a grip, Callie Marie. Everything is fine," I told myself. I quickly showered and gently washed myself since it's been well over two years since I've had sex, and I was sore as hell. I needed to face Nate. I just didn't know what to say. I felt awkward and shy right now. I had sex for the first time in years, and neither of us could remember the deed. It was crazy, no, it was ludicrous! I mean, I'd had full-on erotic dreams about what it would be like having Nate. It finally happened, and I couldn't remember a damn detail!

"Ugh!" I screamed, throwing myself on the bed, inhaling Nate's scent on the pillow he slept on last night. Creeping very slowly and quietly out of my room, I shut my door and tiptoed toward the kitchen, where I saw Nate making French toast with eggs, bacon, and a full pot of coffee brewed and a cup he was sipping on.

"So you're not only worth millions, you cook too?" I laughed.

"Hmm…well, there's a lot you don't know about me, sweets. Come on over here so I can properly say good morning, would ya? I can't leave my food. It'll burn," he said with a wink.

Walking over, I knew my face was bright red, but I couldn't help it. These butterflies he gave me when he talked so sweet got me every time.

"Good morning to you, too, handsome. You do know you didn't have to make breakfast, right?"

"Of course, but what kind of man would I be if I didn't feed my woman after a night like we had?"

"Your woman, and a night like we had?"

"Well, I can't really remember anything besides getting you in and desperately trying to get that annoying-ass jumper off you, but I'm assuming something happened, considering there's a used condom in the trash, and you made comments about being sore. As far as the 'my woman' goes, I'd very much like it if you'd be my girlfriend, Callie. I find you extremely sexy, and my attraction to you is beyond anything I've ever felt toward another woman. My body is screaming at me not to let you go and that I need you with every fiber of my being. So what do you say? Are you willing to give it a try?"

I stood there, staring at this amazing man who had just laid all his cards on the table for me, and I was at a loss for words and what I should do.

"I don't know what to say, Nate. My heart is screaming yes, but my head is screaming, 'Are you sure?' I'm scared. I haven't been in a relationship with anyone except Jake. I don't even know how to do this. I'm sorry I'm so confusing. I don't want to be, I swear, but it's part of my DNA, I guess."

"Just say yes, Callie. What are you scared of?"

"Well, for starters: myself, you, life in general. I don't know how to live life with other people. I've been existing on my own for six almost seven years. How do I change that in a span of a few months? I, I, I don't know, Nate!"

"Look at me, Callie. Have I done anything to make you think or feel sad or bad? Have I once pushed you to do something you're not comfortable with or didn't want to do?"

"No, you haven't. What if something happens? I won't survive losing another person close to me. I won't! I'm so scared of letting anyone else in. Life has this way of taking everything I love and killing it or taking it away indefinitely."

"Baby, look at me, okay? Listen to me when I say this, all right, I am not going anywhere anytime soon. Can I promise you that, well, frankly, no, but what I can promise is that choosing to give this relationship a try will help you get over this fear of losing people. It will help you see that you are not alone and that it's okay to let others in, especially if their name is Nate Owens." He laughed, trying to ease the tension in me. I just sagged against Nate, knowing he was right and that he had won me over for now.

"Okay, Nate, let's try, but if we decide to be intimate again, can we please do it sober so I can at least remember having sex for the first time in well over two years."

Nate busted out laughing. "Of course, beautiful, and I'm really sorry, neither of us can remember last night. Let's eat. The food is getting cold. How do you take your coffee, sweets?"

"One lump of sugar and a bit of sweet cream, please."

"Coming right up, my lady."

Chapter 29

Callie

It'd been a little over six weeks since Nate asked me to be his girlfriend, and let me tell you, being his girlfriend was amazing! He treated me like I was the only person in his world. We'd been on three dates, and every one of them was unique and romantic. He was one of the most genuine and kind people I'd ever had the pleasure of knowing. Every date was so new and different. Nothing was the same. It was always something I'd never seen or had someone do for me before. He got along with Layla extremely well and could deal with her no-filter mouth that she had. Not many people could tolerate her bluntness, even though I struggled at times.

I had embraced myself in the aspect of letting go of my past to heal but never forgetting any of it. Braxton continued to help me improve myself and let go of any of the guilt I held onto from any of it, which reminds me, I see him again in about four hours. I could never thank Nate enough for passing Braxton's information to me. It was probably one of the best things to have happened to me in the past six and a half years. I wasn't feeling very well last week, so I had to reschedule for today, and yet I was still not feeling the best.

"Well, I guess you better get up, Callie Marie," I said to myself. I've been battling this cold for the last week and just haven't felt myself. Last night, I almost vomited. I had such a terrible bitter taste in my mouth. After talking to Layla and Nate last night, I finally fell asleep around midnight. I was exhausted and felt like I hadn't slept in days. I just don't know what's wrong with me. Maybe I should make an appointment with my doctor and get some medicine. I hate being a big baby, but with a busy schedule like mine, I don't have time to be sick.

Hearing my doorbell ring, I quickly got up and raced to the door, opened it, and ran to the sink to puke.

"My god, what's wrong with me, Layla? I never get sick!"

"Girl, I have my suspicions, and I've brought something with me. Before you throw me out over it, hear me out, okay?"

"Umm…that's not the way I'd like to start a conversation," I said while sitting down and laying my head on the table to get the coolness on my face from it.

"I'm too damn tired and sick to throw you out, so just spit it out, all right?"

"Okay, you asked for it, Callie Marie. I bought you a pregnancy test. Now here go. Pee on it," she said, and I damn near fell out of my chair, trying to get to the sink to release anything left of the contents in my stomach.

"Oh, dear god, I'm not pregnant. I've only had sex once in the last two and a half years, and we used a condom."

"Okay, but listen, Callie. You said yourself that neither of you could remember having sex or using the condom. What's the harm in just peeing on the stick? Just humor me, will you? Just this once, please?"

"Okay, but I'm telling you, I'm not pregnant."

"Yeah, I hear you, but I still want you to pee on that stick. Now go hurry up, and when you're done, holler so I can set a timer."

After getting in the bathroom, I sat on the floor, and I was just trying to will myself to pee on this damn thing. I couldn't be pregnant. I've only had sex once, right? We used a condom. It was in the trash. I saw it with my own eyes. No way am I pregnant, please. I can't be pregnant. I don't deserve to be a mother again. "I'm not pregnant," I repeated to myself one more time before I got up and peed on it.

"Okay, Layla, set the timer." I went out and fell on my bed, still praying to myself not to be positive, but the doubts were creeping in. It'd been six weeks since that night. Neither one of us remembered anything beyond getting in the front door. I didn't technically touch the condom, so who's to say it didn't just get opened and thrown in there?

"Oh my god, Layla, what if we had sex more than once? I don't think I can be a mother again. What if the Ativan has caused damage to the baby? Oh my god, I could have caused brain damage to my baby! Oh, dear lord, all the drinking you talk me into, it can cause trouble with the pregnancy and baby too! I'm a terrible mother, and I haven't even birthed this kid yet!"

Layla grabbed my face with both hands and instructed me to take a breath and blew it out. Then she hugged me.

"Callie, listen to me, okay? Everything is going to be okay. If you're pregnant, we'll figure it out together. If you're not, then hey, we'll figure that shit out together too. Either way, I'm here for you. You've got options, and no matter what, you're not stuck in any way, okay? Now let's see this result."

"I'm scared," I cried. "What if I'm pregnant and something happens to this baby? Then what? Will I lose Nate too? I can't lose people like that again. I can't."

"I know you can't, Callie. If anyone understands you, it's me. I was with you through everything. I saw how broken you were with the kid's accident and then Jake's. I will do everything in my power to prevent anything from hurting you ever again. It's my duty as your best friend, but right now, we need to know if you're expecting or not. Do you understand, Callie?"

I just shook my head and let Layla lead me to the bathroom. Layla saw the test first and pulled me into a hug. "It's going to be okay, Callie Marie."

"Is it positive?"

"It is, Callie. I'm so sorry. I know you're scared, but this is a new start to a new life for you, girl."

Too shocked to say anything, I just slowly slid down the wall and buried my face in my knees and cried.

"Come on, Callie. It's going to be okay. Let's get up and get in the shower."

I couldn't even respond to Layla. I was numb and scared, disappointed in myself for not being careful. How could I let this happen?

I couldn't save my children the last time. What makes me different this time? What if Nate thinks I did this on purpose? What if he didn't want children? I don't believe in abortion. What if he breaks up with me? What if he wants full custody and fights me in court? He would win, considering I'm such a mess, and he's seen me have a panic attack in public. What if I lose this baby and then Nate can't deal with the pain of it? I won't survive this time.

"I won't do this again. I can't do this again," I mumbled.

Chapter 30

Callie

Waking up, I heard this annoying beeping sound, and my arm was being held down by something heavy.

"What the hell?" I mumbled, opening my eyes and taking a look around. I realized the beeping was coming from the machine I was attached to, and the heaviness on my arm was from Nate's hand. He was asleep with his head in a very uncomfortable-looking position with his back all hunched since he was way too big for this tiny armchair. I couldn't help myself but let out a soft giggle, which got his attention pretty quickly.

"Hey there, beautiful. How are you feeling?"

"Better, I guess, but what am I doing here in the hospital, Nate?"

"Well, Layla called an ambulance after you had a panic attack and passed out in your bathroom."

"Oh my god, I'm pregnant," I said while placing my hand on my stomach. "Nate, I'm pregnant, and I'm so sorry! I didn't know we were going to have sex that night. I, I didn't realize we hadn't used protection."

"Callie, are you seriously apologizing right now for growing a life inside of you, my child inside of you? I could not be more excited. Am I scared? Hell, yes, but I couldn't see myself having kids with anyone else. You're it for me, and I knew that the day I knocked you down with my door at Bustling Corp. I'm 100 percent in this with you. Do I wish we could have planned it? Absolutely, but apparently, this little life wanted to be created now, and I can't say I'm the least bit upset or sad about it, okay? I want this baby, and I want you.

Please don't ever apologize for getting pregnant. It took both of us that night, and I can promise you, even without remembering the details, that I was a willing participant in any extracurricular activities we practiced that night."

"I love you, Nate," I blurted out and wrapped my hands around his neck. Realizing what I had just said, my heart rate started to beat faster, and that seemed to be all you could hear throughout the entire room. Oh god, he doesn't love me yet, and I've just blurted out the L-word first! Right as I started to panic, I felt Nate's arms wrap around me and a kiss placed in the crook of my neck.

"I didn't know what love was until now, Callie. I've never felt this for any other woman before you. I just thought it was infatuation, but I know now it's love. I wasn't sure what love felt like besides the love you have for your family, but this goes so much above and beyond that. There are so many feelings all the time when I'm around you that feel like they're going to burst right out of me, just exploding me into a million pieces. I love you so much more than I have ever loved another person, and that's a scary thought, I know, but it's the truth. I'm so glad you love me, too, because I wasn't sure how long I could keep that to myself. I was so scared if I told you, it'd scare you away."

"You probably would have." I laughed. "Nate, I can't promise you a happy life, you know. I'm me, and as scary as that is, now we're bringing a life into this mess. Well, I'm the mess. You're more like a hot part of my mess that I like the best right now."

Nate put a finger on my lips and said, "Shh, no more rambling, beautiful. I'm going to kiss you now so I can show you how happy and in love with you I am."

Finally I got discharged with clear instructions to drink plenty of water and rest for the next several days. A smile was formed on my face. I won't lie and say having Nate by my side didn't help that smile. Do I still have reservations about this new life forming inside of me? Quite frankly, yes, but I believe Nate when he said he'd be by my side through it all, and for some reason, that helped reassure me more than anything. I never thought in a gazillion years that I would end up with a wonderful boyfriend and another baby on the way. I thought that I had lost everything good in my life and that I deserved to barely survive this world for the rest of my days. Instead, life threw a curveball my way in the form of Nate Owens. I couldn't imagine my life without Nate in it now. It's like we were always in each other's lives and that we've been best friends and lovers for years, even though we haven't done anything in the form of intimacy since that night six weeks ago. I guess we just decided we'd know when the time was right, and it just hasn't felt right yet. I am so crazy in love with this man that I'm not sure if it's obsession or just pure infatuation. He's amazing in every way honestly. He goes above and beyond any of my life's dreams of a second part to me and my life. I couldn't imagine doing this life without him now. I need him forever, and I hope that this new life we're working on creating together will be kind to us and to our future children because, for the life of me, this is the first time I have felt like doing anything besides barely surviving.

"I love you, Nate," I said and reached up to give him a sweet, gentle, but passionate kiss.

"What was that for, beautiful?"

"You brought me back to life, Nate, and it's for showing me there's more to life after my past than just barely surviving, Nate, and I couldn't love you more for that."

Epilogue

"Okay, big breath, Callie, and hold it. Now push to ten, okay?"

"One, two, three, four, five, six, seven, eight, ahhhhh. Oh my god, I can't do this! Give me drugs. I changed my mind. Please, I want the epidural."

"Listen to me, Callie. It's too late for the epidural now. I need you to push. We have to get the baby out. Now big breath, in and bare down to ten."

"Here we go. It's okay, baby, I'm right here. I've got you, beautiful. Just push, okay? You're almost done. She's here. I can see her head. Oh my god, I can see her head," Nate said, and the doctor asked the nurse to please bring the dad a chair.

"I don't need a chair. I'm good," he said.

"Are you sure? You look a little pale, Nate," I said.

"I'm fine, beautiful. You're doing so good."

"Oh god, here comes another one. Nate, please help me, god, it hurts so bad!"

"Big breath, Callie, and push, 1, 2, 3, 4, 5, 6—okay, Callie, breathe through the pain, don't push the heads out. Okay, now gentle push, Callie. That's it, and there she is, Mommy!" The whole room burst with a baby's screams and cries.

"She's beautiful, Callie."

"She looks like Savannah, Nate." I burst into tears. "She looks like my sweet girl. How is that possible? It's like looking at a clone of her, Nate."

"Callie, you are their mother, so, of course, it's possible she's perfect, just like you."

"Okay, Callie, here comes another one. Get ready to push."

The nurse grabbed my daughter to begin cleaning her up so I could deliver my daughter's twin.

"I don't think I want any more children, Nate!" I screamed at the top of my lungs while grabbing his shirt and yanking his head next to mine.

He kissed my nose and said, "Whatever you decide, beautiful!"

"Why are you always so calm, dammit? Ah, oh my god, it burns so bad. Get him out now!" I screamed while pushing as hard as I could.

"And breathe, Callie, the head is out. Just let me get this cord unwrapped from his neck, and there we go now. Gentle push, and there he is, a beautiful bouncing baby boy with quite the set of lungs."

"Wow, much louder than his sister," Nate said.

"He's perfect, Nate, ten fingers, ten toes. He looks like you but has my Dustin's nose."

"He's beautiful, Callie, and thank you for bringing my children into this world, making me a father. I can never thank you enough. You're my life, you know, and I love you so much, my sweets."

"I love you, too, Nate. Now can you go check on our daughter? I'd like to hold her."

"I'm going to take him, Mrs. Palet, get him cleaned up, and bring him back to you in a few minutes."

"All right, thank you."

"Your daughter weighs seven pounds and six ounces, nineteen and a half inches long."

"Look at you, my sweet sugarplum. You're beautiful," I softly whispered to her while caressing her face.

"She's so awake and alert. Is that normal?" Nate asked.

"Well, all babies are different, Mr. Owens, and the fact that Mom didn't use any medication for pain control means the baby doesn't have any of that to course through their bloodstream either. They'll sleep in a bit, though most babies do sleep for a while after being born. Here's your son. He weighs eight pounds, two ounces, and is twenty-one inches long."

"Oh, you sweet boy, look at you trying to outdo your sister. Yes, you are," I cooed. "You want to hold your daughter, Nate?"

"I do. Can someone just make sure I'm doing it right?" He laughed. "I've only ever held one baby, and I was sixteen years old, so I may be a bit rusty."

"Yeah, like rusty is the correct word to use," I said while laughing. "Just like this, babe. Support her head. Yeah, just like that. There ya go, a natural, Nate."

"Hello there, baby girl! I'm your dad. I'm going to keep all the boys away and keep you safe for the rest of your life, even when you're an adult. I've waited a long time to meet you and your brother. You know you could have been a little easier on your mom though."

Waking up, I heard Nate talking to the babies, so I just lay there listening for a few minutes.

"You know, if we just give Mommy a few more minutes of sleep, I'm sure she'll wake up, and you can eat as much as you want. Mommy and I have waited so long to meet you both, you know. We loved you from the moment the stick showed two pink lines. That was before we realized there were two of you. You have two siblings in heaven, and I know Mommy will have many stories to share with you about them when you're older. I'm sure they would have loved having a baby brother and sister."

I rolled over at that with tears in my eyes. "Have I told you lately how much I love you, Nate?"

"Not since yesterday, but I'll definitely listen to you say it again because I am so in love with you and these two babies we've created together."

"I love you, Nate Michael Owens, so much more than I could ever show you!"

"And I love you, Callie Marie Palet! Which baby you want to feed first? You probably should start with our baseball player here since he is trying to eat anything that gets near his mouth." Nate laughed. After getting my son latched on and eating, I turned to Nate.

"So I was thinking, what about Micah Levi Owens and Leah Elizabeth Owens?"

"I love them, Callie, and I think they're perfect! Hey there, little Leah, how's daddy's sweet girl this morning, huh?" Nate cooed. After feeding the babies, we finally got discharge papers, and they made me sit in a wheelchair, claiming hospital policy.

"Okay, beautiful, we just have one place to stop on the way home."

"What? Where would we need to stop, Nate? I don't want the babies out very long."

"I know, sweets, and I promise after this stop, we'll go straight home."

"Okay, Nate." Pulling up, I realized Nate had brought me to the hot springs and waterfall from our first date.

"Nate, why are we here?"

"Well, get out and come find out, would ya?" he teased with a wink and walked down the path, leaving me to wonder how I'd get the babies out of the car and down the path by myself.

"Nate, Nate, what is going on? Hey, girl, what's up? Layla? What are you doing here?"

"Well, girly, I'm going to watch my beautiful god niece and handsome godson, duh! Now get down the path and be careful. Can't have the new mom injured." Layla laughed.

Kissing my babies and making Layla promise to call me if they made one single peep, I started the short walk down the path. Coming up on the hot springs, I noticed Katie standing there.

"Hey, what are you doing here, Kate?"

"What, Callie, I'm not here. Just keep walking, and you'll find who you're looking for a few steps further."

I walked around the corner of the trees, and there I saw my Nate, standing looking out at the waterfall surrounded by roses of all different colors in the shape of a heart. There are probably a hundred tea-light candles lit all around the entire area. In the middle of the heart is a jewelry box open, and in it is the most gorgeous ring I've ever seen before. I looked up at Nate, who was now in that heart on one knee looking at me.

"Hey, beautiful, I've wanted to do this for a really long time now and just haven't found the right time. Callie, I knew from the moment I saw you on the floor rubbing your forehead after I knocked you down with my door that you were my forever, the person I wanted to spend the rest of my life with. I have watched you blossom from a woman who was so badly broken inside with little confidence to this amazing, happy, extremely proud woman. I have prayed many hours to God to give you strength and courage to overcome your past and become my future. When you brought Micah and Leah into this world, I knew this was the right time for me to ask you to be my wife. You have made me the happiest I have ever been in my entire life, Callie Marie, and I hope that you'll let me make you happy for the rest of our lives together. Callie Marie Palet, will you do me the honor of becoming my wife?"

"Oh my god, Nate, yes!" I said, shaking my head yes, and threw my arms around his neck, kissing his face all over with tears pouring down my face. "I love you, Nate, so much! I haven't been so filled with love in so long, and I'm so thankful to God for bringing you into my life and giving me Micah and Leah!"

"I can't wait for the rest of our lives together, Callie Marie Palet, soon-to-be Callie Marie Owens!"

"Me neither, Nate, and you're the best thing to have come into my life in the last seven years, and I couldn't imagine just barely surviving anymore. I had no idea what was in store for me when I accepted Bustling Corps renovation request, but I am so thankful our paths crossed, Nate!"

Nate handed me a glass of grape juice and himself a glass of bubbly. "Here's to our future and many, many more years together!"

About the Author

Christina Stuebs was born in 1982 in Illinois. She is a wife of twenty-six years and a mother to eight amazing children, tragically losing two of those children in a camping accident. She knew she wanted to write books as a little girl but never followed through until now. She wanted to share her story with the world, compelling others to see that grief is hard and that it truly takes time to overcome the traumas that follow that loss. Not everything in the book is true since her husband is here today and supports her in any way he can. She says the men in her story are both her husband, the husband she had right after their loss, and the husband she perceives she has today. She hopes you enjoy her very first novel, *Barely Surviving*.

Printed in the USA
CPSIA information can be obtained
at www.ICGtesting.com
CBHW030135041024
15319CB00043B/406